Praise for the Ruby, the Rabbi's Wife mysteries . . .

Hold the Cream Cheese, Kill the Lox

"Agatha-nominee Sharon Kahn's 'kosher kozies' have a charm all their own . . . The antics of self-centered Essie Sue Margolis, who's fussing over the impending bar mitzvah of her obnoxious twin cousins, provide plenty of comic relief." —*Publishers Weekly*

Don't Cry for Me, Hot Pastrami

"Energy and good humor . . . Fast and fun from beginning to end." —*Booklist*

"A fast-paced mystery, a cast of quirky characters, [and] humor and wit that will make readers giggle if not laugh out loud . . . Delightful." —*Publishers Weekly*

"Much humor." —*Library Journal*

Never Nosh a Matzo Ball

"A rare treat." —Susan Wittig Albert

"Kahn helps readers to a full serving of Judaic wit and wisdom in this follow-up cozy to *Fax Me a Bagel*." —*Publishers Weekly*

"A cast of endearing characters and liberal amounts of comic relief." —*Ottawa Citizen*

"Plenty of memorable characters." —*Kirkus Reviews*

continued . . .

Fax Me a Bagel

"Sit down with a garlic bagel, schmear it with cream cheese and sliced lox, and read this book . . . it's pure joy."
—Alan M. Dershowitz, author of *Chutzpah*

"The history of the bagel, a hilarious congregation, and true-blue friends fill the subplots and combine with a first-rate puzzle . . . excellent entertainment."
—*The Dayton Jewish Observer*

"Effectively combines humor with crime. Expect more from Ruby the rabbi's wife."
—*Booklist*

"A heroine with heart, soul, and an unfailing sense of humor . . . Kahn captures life in a small Texas town with warmth and insight . . . a terrific new voice."
—Deborah Crombie, Edgar Award–nominated author of *Dreaming of the Bones*

"Entertaining . . . The action unfolds at a smart pace . . . A welcome addition to the ranks of amateur female sleuths."
—*Publishers Weekly*

"Ruby . . . has just been declared my new best friend. She's a hoot. Collard greens and bagels? It doesn't get much better, y'all."
—Anne George, Agatha Award–winning author of *Murder on a Girl's Night Out*

"A saucy puzzler with a side order of zesty characters . . . a slam-bang good time."
—Nancy Bell, Agatha Award–nominated author of *Biggie and the Fricasseed Fat Man*

hold the cream cheese,

Kill the Lox

sharon kahn

BERKLEY PRIME CRIME, NEW YORK

HOLD THE CREAM CHEESE, KILL THE LOX

A Berkley Prime Crime Book / published by arrangement with Scribner, a division of Simon & Schuster Inc.

PRINTING HISTORY
Scribner hardcover edition / September 2002
Berkley Prime Crime mass-market edition / August 2003

ISBN: 0-425-19131-1

Berkley Prime Crime Books are published
by The Berkley Publishing Group,
a division of Penguin Group (USA) Inc.,
375 Hudson Street, New York, New York 10014.
The name BERKLEY PRIME CRIME
and the BERKLEY PRIME CRIME design
are trademarks belonging to Penguin Group (USA) Inc.

PRINTED IN THE UNITED STATES OF AMERICA

10 9 8 7 6 5 4 3 2 1

In Memory of Anne George

acknowledgments
···

To my family and mainstays as Ruby marches on: David, Suzy, Jon, Emma, and Camille Weizenbaum, Nancy Nussbaum, Ruthe Winegarten, Suzanne and Ned Bloomfield, Lindsy Van Gelder, Pamela Brandt, Nancy Hendrickson, and Kathi Stein.

To the Shoal Creek Writers: Judith Austin Mills, Karen Casey Fitzjerrell, Dena Garcia, Eileen Joyce, and Nancy Bell.

Special thanks to Helen Rees of the Helen Rees Agency and to Susanne Kirk, vice president and executive editor of Scribner, for their invaluable help and encouragement, and to Erik Wasson, Dena Rosenberg, and Angella Baker of Scribner, Joan Mazmanian of the Helen Rees Agency, and all those at Scribner who helped guide the book along its way.

My great appreciation to Charlene Crilley for Ruby's Web site, *www.sharonkahn.com*.

prologue

The ivory-handled knife was sharp, and the twin salmon pieces, center cut, glistened on his cutting board with the color of fire opals. The old man's cronies in the trade would have said the salmon was alive—an endearment reserved only for the freshest and most supple fillets. The prize before him, however, had not come from the Brooklyn smokehouses of his prime—in fact, it was not smoked at all. The delicacy he was about to slice on the diagonal and away from the skin was gravlax, cured by using kosher salt and sugar.

Three days ago he had carefully dried the two fillets with a paper towel, placing one fillet skin side down in a square Pyrex glass dish. Before laying the other piece, sandwich-style, on top of the first with the skin side up, he made a filling of salt, sugar, and crushed white peppercorns, topping the mixture with fresh dill after he spread it. He covered the whole structure with plastic wrap and then used a heavy pewter tray to mash it down. He placed it on a roomy refrigerator shelf, and piled four washed bricks on top of the covering tray. Now, all the juices could squeeze through the flesh and marinate in harmony, disturbed only once every twelve hours when he dismantled the bricks, turned the fish over in the dish to thoroughly absorb the flavors, and weighted it down again.

The gravlax, prepared at a table on his back porch in the heart of Central Texas, was now ready once again to showcase the skilled cutting technique he had perfected so many years before. He had only a few hours before his appointment at The Hot Bagel. On this occasion, he would command a greater fee than he had the first time for the *simchah*—the special religious event followed by the feast he so expertly provided. This gravlax was an even more elegant example of what he could prepare at the Temple for the guests to enjoy after the ceremony.

The front doorbell rang, and he went to answer it, wiping his hands on a paper towel as he walked. He opened the door and looked around. He saw no one. He walked outside. Nothing. After a few seconds he closed the door, relieved to continue preparing his gravlax without interruption. He returned through the kitchen to the screened porch to unwrap the fish for cutting, glad that any odors could escape in the cool open air. He sat down at the table again, and reached for his knife.

It was gone.

chapter
1

....

"Twins beget twins, Ruby. I thought you knew that."

"Why would I know that, Essie Sue? And especially before I've had my coffee."

"The Bible says so. In Genesis."

The woman is many things, but never unsure. Where does this kind of certainty come from—is it genetic? What I do know is that the Bible says no such thing.

"I'm explaining to you, Ruby, that my second cousin, Rae Bitman, one of the Bitman twins of Buda, is the mother of these two delightful twin boys, and that the twinship came through the female side."

"I'm glad you cleared that up. And you don't need to say two twins—it's redundant."

I should have let that pass, but if I can manage to irritate her, maybe she'll leave. She's already destroyed my favorite part of the morning—when I sit out on my deck with the *Times* and a steaming mug of freshly ground Sumatra and slowly come alive.

"Always contrary, Ruby, but I'm going to ignore that.

Rabbi Kapstein can settle Genesis for us later—the clergy have to study all the generations as part of their training."

Oh, right. Kevin, our current rabbi at Temple Rita, avoids the begets and begots like the plague—he says it makes him dizzy. But this is the second argument in a row Essie Sue has passed up since she arrived here at seven-thirty, and it really has me worried. On top of which, she's found several excuses to wander around inside the house, and I can't figure out what she's looking for. Even here on Watermelon Lane, a giant step down in the local real estate chain from neighborhoods like hers, we don't make a habit of visiting each other when it's barely light outside.

I should mention that Essie Sue Margolis, still the rock and pillar of our small congregation here in Eternal, has never given up her unending goal of molding me into the perfect rabbi's wife, even though the rabbi in question, my husband, Stu, died quite a few years ago. But I thought my status as a single woman had discouraged the pop-in visits she used to make when Stu was on the payroll.

"So what about the Bitman twins from Buda, Essie Sue?" (Buda, by the way, is pronounced *B-YEW-da* by those of us not new to Central Texas.) "All I know about them is that you enlisted them to take poor Professor Gonzales's body home before our unfortunate temple fundraising cruise departed from Galveston last year."

"I'm trying to tell you, Ruby—Rae Bitman, the oldest twin by three minutes, is married to Harold Levee of Buda."

"You mean Levy?"

"No, Levee, as in down on the levee to New Orleans. It's actually nicer than Levy, don't you think?"

I don't let myself think in these situations—it's safer.

"They have twelve-year-old twin boys who will be thirteen next spring, Ruby."

"There's no arguing with that."

"Since they're family and live so far away, I'm insisting that Lester and Larry Levee be Bar Mitzvahed in the Jewish tradition, even though their mother thinks graduation at Buda Middle School is enough ceremony for one year. I'm driving the rabbi down to talk to them."

"Isn't it a little late? Bar Mitzvah training usually takes a few years. And Buda's not that far away."

"It's far enough, and this is a special case. They can have an abbreviated course."

"Kevin thinks this is okay?"

Why I expected an answer to this is beside the point.

"The religious part is the rabbi's responsibility—mine is the lunch."

"Beg pardon?"

"I certainly want them welcomed in the right way, Ruby. And they wear huskies, so I need to shop in Austin for their outfits—we don't have any Big and Talls for children here in Eternal."

"Aren't you getting ahead of yourself? They might grow out of the huskies in a year."

"It's never too early for fashion. You'll love the boys, though. They're adorable. They have the cutest curly locks—just like when they were babies. And they're just as spirited."

"Spirited?" This is not a word Essie Sue uses lightly.

"You know—enthusiastic. The lovable Levee twins, their parents call them."

"And everybody else calls them?"

"Ruby, quit speculating. You don't even know them."

"But you do, right? And why are you telling me?"

I'm getting a hard knot in the pit of my stomach.

"I slipped a tape measure into my purse this morning, and I took a quick look-see at your guest room, Ruby. It's quite large."

"But definitely not large enough for the lovable Levees, Essie Sue."

"Only on weekends until the end of the year."

"In your dreams."

Or my nightmares.

chapter
2

·····················

"Watch that piece of Swiss, Ruby—it's awfully thick."

"Huh? You're kidding, right?"

I'm gazing at the folded piece of Swiss cheese I've just put on top of a pumpernickel bagel still hot from the oven. It looks perfectly normal to me. But whenever Milt Aboud—my business partner here at The Hot Bagel—gets a little weird, I know it's money-related.

"I told you the costs in the deli have gone up astronomically lately—it's killing me. I just don't want you to overdo it on the cheese—I can't control the expenses like I do the bagels. Eat as many of those as you want."

"Uh—correct me if I'm wrong, Miltie, but aren't you talking about *our* deli? And last time I looked, I had a part-interest in the bagels, too—not that I ever intend to eat as many as I want. You know where that could get me."

Milt often forgets we're partners. He's operated The Hot Bagel in our little town of Eternal, Texas, for more years than he chooses to remember, and I became an investor in the business only a few years ago after my husband, Stu, died. My meager profits from this deal, plus the fluctuating income I get from winging it as a computer consultant, are all that are keeping me afloat. Of course, I could always get a regular job involving a boss and other odious options, but that would blunt the drama of never knowing where my next paycheck is coming from. Besides, I have a horrible time with subservience, as my former teachers will attest to.

"Sorry, Ruby, I guess I overreached with the cheese slices. But wait'll you look at this month's invoices—especially the meats and fish. I've gotten the brush-off all month from Rocko, the distributor. He won't talk about the price hikes."

"We have a distributor named Rocko? That's our first mistake, wouldn't you say? Our books say they're Acme Jobbers, Inc., of Seattle and Kodiak."

"That's Rocko. His standards have always been high, until lately. The salmon's slightly tougher these days, and the color's not the same. I think he's charging more money for lesser-quality goods."

"Then, let's change suppliers."

"It's not that easy—Rocko's got the best connections, and these guys can be pretty competitive. I've made some overtures to other people, and I've sensed a distinct lack of enthusiasm for taking over his customers. I'm gonna track him down and talk to him about this, but I'm afraid it's a setup for our paying even higher prices for the best products. We might have to come up with more money."

"Okay, let's both pursue this. I'll do some general cost comparisons, and you handle the specifics with Rocko. We might just have to raise prices, if the whole market is rising."

"That's not going to solve the short-term problem, Ruby—it's possible we'll have to come up with some money up front."

"*Oy.* I knew what I was investing in when I went into this, Milt, but I didn't count on unexpected expenses."

"I didn't count on them, either—believe me. I just wanted to tell you so you'd be prepared."

"Prepared to rob a bank, maybe—this is a tight time for me."

"Well, it hasn't happened yet—I still have to talk to Acme Jobbers. Meanwhile, we need to cater more parties—you said you'd work on the outside stuff."

"Absolutely."

"I think you should stick around for your friend Essie Sue's meeting today with that retired lox slicer from New York."

"But that party's not until next spring—months from now. We could be buried six feet under by then."

"Don't try to get out of it, Ruby. You know how I get when I'm around her, and we can't really afford to turn anyone off. You seem to be able to deal with her."

"Me? Where did you get that? Not from anyone we know, certainly. Besides, I've been avoiding her because she wants me to do her a favor I can refuse and, so far, have refused."

"Sounds ominous."

"You can't imagine. It concerns the Bar Mitzvah boys."

"My Bar Mitzvah boys, Ruby?" It's Essie Sue. "My grand-cousins Larry and Lester? What concerns them?"

Essie Sue Margolis is the only person I know who, in one swoop, can assail a room, commandeer a table, eavesdrop on the nearest conversation, and magnetize all subsequent events so that they revolve solely around her.

"Oh, just preparing for your meeting today. Milt asked me to stick around."

"For what reason? I didn't ask either of you to be here—you'll just get in the way of my interview with Herman Guenther. You know him, Ruby, from the Temple. He's auditioning for the position of lox maven at the boys' Bar Mitzvah. He provides his own lox."

"You're calling the boys your grand-cousins? Is that part of the language?"

"Well, if it isn't, it should be—it cuts through all that once-removed business."

"You may have something there. And can you say that again about Herman's being the lox maven? This is something one auditions for?"

"Of course. I'm hiring him as a professional—to come up with something totally unique in the way of lox presentation. If he can cut, he can sculpt, yes? Fish decoration is his specialty, and what's a Bar Mitzvah table without a lovely lox? His granddaughter is in Larry's and Lester's Bar Mitzvah year—they'll have some classes together."

"Herman works with us on catering sometimes. He shouldn't have to audition. He catered the Copeland wedding six months ago, so you already know he's good—they loved him."

"They might have loved him, but I don't trust the Copelands. They criticized the illustrated article I wrote for the *Eternal Ear* about the wedding, remember—the one with all the photographs? Just because I made that innocent remark about the bride's nose job. Taking all those photos also kept me too busy to sample the lox—the platter was empty by the time I got to it."

"Maybe you have the lox before the horse, Essie Sue. The boys haven't even begun studying yet, and you're already into the food."

"And food is our specialty, Ruby," Milt says. "If Mr. Guenther provides the lox, we can cater the rest of the spread."

Oh no. Don't tell me Milt's groveling—he must really be hard up. And what's worse, Essie Sue notices. She can't stand him, but that's not going to stop her from taking him on as a new acolyte.

I see what's coming, but there's nothing I can do to stop it. "Thank you, Milt, for appreciating my business. And did your partner Ruby happen to tell you that she turned down a lucrative and perfectly wonderful opportunity to get to know my exceptional grand-cousins close up?"

chapter
3

······················

E-mail from: Nan
To: Ruby
Subject: *You're Doing What?*

Ruby, are you out of your mind? You've finally joined the human race after years of mourning Stu, you have an adorable boyfriend who I'm assuming has normal impulses, and you're planning on telling him that twelve-year-old twin boys will be bouncing on your bed every weekend? And why can't Essie Sue keep them?

And don't be tied up with the kids for too long. I had plans for us in November—I was just waiting for confirmation. I'm serving on a law committee with business in Alaska! We could both go. It'd be a real adventure. We could tramp around and see all sorts of stuff outside the cities—places I wouldn't visit on my own.

···

E-mail from: Ruby
To: Nan
Subject: *Take It Easy*

How long have you and I been friends—since grad school, right? Our babies grew up like siblings. And who talked you into becoming a lawyer? So give me a break here— I'm suffering enough as it is. Essie Sue told Milt I'd refused her offer to let the twins stay with me, and then she mentioned for the first time that she was going to make this a business deal. She must have sniffed out that we needed money the minute Milt broke tradition and said a nice word to her. When he heard this meant real cash, he looked so pitiful I couldn't say no. Also, she said I don't have to baby-sit the kids—she's doing that at her house, and they'll only be sleeping here.

As for Ed, I wouldn't exactly call him my boyfriend. I mean maybe we aren't seeing other people, but if so, it's not part of any commitment. He's going to Mexico on assignment for the paper in San Antonio. If we want time alone before that, I'll go to San Antonio and Essie Sue can get someone to stay here with the boys. She can't let them spend nights with her because Hal had that heart episode this fall and the doctor wants him to have uninterrupted sleep. What she does with them during the day is her problem, not mine. She says Kevin's helping her, although I doubt that she's informed him. I can even recruit Milt if I have to, now that he's put the pressure on me.

I'm trying to look at the good side of this. How bad can they be? Don't forget, I'm used to boys. It's been a long time since Joshie was home, and I miss his loud music and the sound of his basketball hitting the driveway. Call me nostalgic.

I'd love to think about Alaska, but I'll have to wait until later to see if I can afford it. If work picks up and I can help

Milt solve the bakery's financial problems, who knows?
Can you hold off?

••

E-mail from: Nan
To: Ruby
Subject: *I Give Up*

Okay, I can accept your keeping the kids as business, but
I still think you'll be sorry.

And I won't count on your coming with me to Alaska,
but don't forget you can stay in the room with me if you
decide to make the trip.

So how was the lox maven? Did he strut his stuff?

••

E-mail from: Ruby
To: Nan
Subject: *Maven*

He never showed up.

chapter
4

....

"Boys, don't gang up on the rabbi."

We're in the rabbi's study, where Lester and Larry Levee
have just wrestled Kevin to the ground, or I should say, to
the Moroccan rug purchased by the Goodman family—at-
tested to by the bronze plaque affixed to one corner by
brads. After a vain attempt to escape by rolling under his
enormous rococo desk, Kevin has given up and lies there,
Gulliver-like, while the twins proclaim victory by sitting
on his legs.

"It's your own fault, Rabbi," Essie Sue continues, "you
should never have accepted their challenge to play WWF."

"I didn't know WWF meant World Wrestling Federa-
tion. I'm not good at that. I thought it had something to do
with one of the World Wars."

"It obviously did," I say. "Get off him, you losers."

The word *losers* makes a dent—the first one of the afternoon. Apparently, the twins are shocked by my suggestion
that they aren't winners, when Kevin is so clearly flattened
beneath them. They give me an offended look and go to
seek the protection of their cousin Essie Sue.

"Go help him up," I tell them, "this is a grown-up you've squashed."

Kevin gets to his knees, has the boys bend over, and hoists himself up by putting a hand on each of their backs. Not the best initiation to scholarly pursuits—he's supposed to be introducing the twins to Judaic studies.

"Boys will be boys," the Cliché Queen assures us. "This will all be forgotten on their Bar Mitzvah day."

I can see already that nothing is going to deter Essie Sue from yet another elaborate production.

"I'm tripling the rent if they stay at my house."

"Don't be silly, Ruby—just growing pains. By the time they finish their stay here in Eternal, they'll have matured and mellowed."

And they'd be ready to be tried as adults, no doubt. Part of me is dying to get hold of these kids—the totally unrealistic part. On the other hand, I've killed an afternoon coming over here to meet them, and I'd like to leave.

"Let's pretend none of this ever happened. What were you planning to do with them today?" I ask Kevin.

"Drill them on the Hebrew letters."

Lester and Larry look alarmed to a sufficient degree that I'm no longer worried about their escaping punishment for accosting Kevin. I had hoped they'd have a more interesting introduction to Jewish learning, but who's to say? The boys might have just met their match.

Essie Sue pulls two chairs in front of Kevin's desk. "Why don't you get to know the twins first, Rabbi?"

Good thinking. Kevin's people skills are somewhere on the level of Larry's and Lester's.

"Okay. Do you guys have any questions about your Bar Mitzvah training?"

Larry has turned his chair backward and is riding it. "Cousin Essie Sue told us we couldn't be Bar Mitzvahed in our cowboy boots. How come?"

"Because your thirteenth birthday is the day when you

become a man, and you're supposed to dress like one on the pulpit. I wear black wing tips, myself." Kevin sticks out his foot.

"I don't think they have wing tips in Buda—at least, I've never seen any like those. What would happen if I wore my boots—would I get damned to hell?"

"We don't get damned to hell in Judaism."

"My friend told me Jews aren't going to heaven, and that there's only one other place to go. Can you guarantee me I won't?"

"Why don't we begin the Hebrew letters now? We'll get into this other stuff later." Kevin brings out a big alphabet chart.

"Good idea, Rabbi." Essie Sue's fantasy of the Levees bonding with Kevin is fading fast.

Lester jumps up. "You haven't let me ask my question yet."

"Let him ask, Rabbi. You have to be fair with twins—I read about this. If not, they can run amok later."

Later? I'm ready to run for the hills now.

"Hurry up, Lester," Kevin says. "What's your question?"

"Do you have a candy jar?"

"What?"

"You know—a candy jar, like in our doctor's office. You're kind of like him, aren't you?"

"The boys are used to getting candy from their pediatrician, Rabbi. You'll have to explain the difference to them."

I look at Kevin. "And you're giving them the abbreviated Bar Mitzvah prep?"

"Don't discourage the rabbi, Ruby—you're always so pessimistic. I think we should go now and leave these men to scholarship."

"Like the difference between a rabbi and a pediatrician? Lots of luck."

"You're not forgetting that you promised to go to the lox

slicer's house with me, are you?" she asked. "I've never even heard of that neighborhood he lives in, and I'm relying on your directions. I can't even get him on the phone."

"I remember." I wouldn't be surprised at anyone who refused to take Essie Sue's phone calls. But at this point, I'll drive her anywhere if it means getting out of here.

The boys look slightly panicked. "Can we go to the lox slicer, too?" Larry says.

"You'll be fine here, children," Essie Sue says. "You'll have a lovely time with the rabbi, and I'll pick you up later."

"How much later?" Kevin yells at our backs.

We make a fast escape before they have time to follow us, leaving Kevin pointing at the letter chart and the boys playing tag. A candy jar might not have been such a bad idea.

chapter
5

....

"We'll take my Lincoln," Essie Sue decrees.

It's fine with me. I don't need her putting down Kleenex before she sits in my front seat. My car was just cleaned inside and out, but reality wouldn't stop her. I always feel like sleeping when I travel in leather-lined luxury, and I begin dozing off despite her steady yakking.

"Pay attention, Ruby—we're coming to the unfamiliar area." The unfamiliar area is one of several working-class neighborhoods she chooses not to be aware of. Herman Guenther lives in a small house on a semi-commercial street, only a half block from Dad's, one of Eternal's most popular breakfast places—the leftover sixties kind—and my favorite blend of hippie and Southern.

I don't know Herman well, but I liked him as soon as I met him at services last year. He must be in his seventies, because he spoke of growing up in prewar Germany, in a village not too far from the northeast coastal towns. He's been in the food business forever and couldn't resist putting off full retirement when he realized that Eternal and Austin could give him enough catering work to supplement his pension. He shows that perfect blend of humor and savvy I find so rare and appealing in men his age, with a touch of shyness thrown in.

Milt likes him, too, and of course he has lots in common with us through the deli connection. We've enjoyed working with him occasionally on catering jobs, and I've dropped off orders at his house from time to time. I can see why he's ignoring Essie Sue's decree that he audition—it's a slap in the face for a seasoned pro like Herman. I'm glad I'm here to be a buffer.

"How do you get the nerve, Essie Sue? You're not representing the *Michelin Guide*. No wonder you haven't heard from Herman."

"People are lax these days, Ruby. If I can catch him at home, he won't be able to avoid me."

Oy. Who can? "Well, at least go easy on the man."

The scraggly yard doesn't stick out here—this is not the manicured section of town. Essie Sue parks the Lincoln in the narrow driveway and picks her way through the gravel in her high heels. We step up on the front porch and ring the bell several times. No answer.

"Let's go around to the back and knock," I say. "At his age, he might be hard of hearing." Although with the racket we've made already, it's more likely that he's simply not home.

"You go, Ruby—I'll wait here."

She never admits that her stilettos are anything but objects of style and beauty, when in fact they're lethal. It's a miracle she hasn't broken an ankle long before now. Or on second thought, she's probably smart enough to let other people—like me—do the walking for her.

I crunch the dried grass as I head for the back of the house. I can see a wide screened porch as I approach. Better give warning so I don't frighten him, or get myself killed. Who knows—he might have adopted the flip side of Texas hospitality and bought a gun for intruders like me.

Before I can call out for Herman, I hear a faint rustle and suddenly confront a growling Doberman, with a collar but, unfortunately, no leash. It could be a neighbor's dog or Herman's, but he's not happy.

I stay still, and then take infinitesimal steps to go back to the side of the house. I've forgotten whether you're supposed to look dogs in the eye or avoid their eyes. As a dog owner, I should know, but I'm not exactly thinking too clearly.

I don't like being here, even if it was my idea. Why am I intruding on behalf of Essie Sue, who's here for no good reason anyway? It's not worth either a dog bite or giving Herman a heart attack from shock.

The Doberman advances as I look away and slouch casually backward, touching the house with one hand for security. It's casual, all right—I run right into a doorjamb and almost trip. The doorjamb is part of an entrance leading from the house to the side yard, and it's ajar. I jump inside and close the door just as the dog leaps forward.

When I catch my breath, I yell out, "Mr. Guenther? Herman?" I want to give plenty of notice, now that I'm an official intruder. And if he does have a heart attack from all this, I'll probably be joining him—my chest is about to break open.

"Ruby? Is that you? Where are you?"

Unfortunately it's Essie Sue, not Herman. I tell her to stay where she is and I'll let her in. No use having her tempt the Doberman on the side of the house.

It's dark inside after the bright sunlight, and I feel my way toward Essie Sue's voice at the front step.

I let her in quickly and shut the door behind her.

"You wouldn't want to know," I say before she can finish her question. No use bringing the subject of dogs into this. "If the doorbells and the yelling haven't flushed him out, he's obviously not home."

"We should at least look around, Ruby. And leave him a note in the kitchen."

"Why the kitchen?"

"Because that's where people go when they come home."

I know better than to argue. Meanwhile, I'm looking around the living room while she's finding the kitchen. Mr. Guenther is a reader—the walls are lined with shelves holding well-worn books. He either buys his at secondhand sales or he's had them for a long time. My usual habit would be to obsessively devour all the titles to see what he reads, but I'm uncomfortable enough just being here. I do look at a table full of photographs—new color pictures of his grandchildren mixed with sepia landscapes from long ago.

Before I can start daydreaming about where he grew up, I hear what can only be described as a crooked croak coming from the other end of the house. I have to listen intently to understand that the croak is being repeated, but faintly. I think it's coming from Essie Sue, but I can't be sure.

Finally, I hear a "Ruby" whispered hoarsely.

"Is that you, Essie Sue? I can't make out what you're saying."

All I get is silence now, so I make my way in the direction of what should be the kitchen area. I go through a bright, sunny kitchen, which, from its warmth and homeyness, must be the true center of the house. I guess Essie Sue was right to leave her note here.

"Ruby."

The croak again, as if there isn't enough breath to form the word.

I follow the sound to the back screened porch off the kitchen. Essie Sue is leaning against the screen. She's not a heavy person, but even so, the flimsy metal screening looks as if it's about to pop out to the backyard from the weight of her body against it. Her eyes are on a large, wooden table where Herman Guenther is slumped over the tabletop, his head resting on his arms.

A slicing knife is in his back.

chapter
6

....

A very compassionate policewoman sits us down in the living room and places big mugs of tea in our hands. Essie Sue is still shaking—I'm sorry she was alone when she found Herman's body on the porch. On the other hand, the snarling Doberman I had to maneuver in the backyard would have really done her in. As for me, I'm having a hard time believing that lovely old man is dead.

"Lieutenant Lundy said he'd be here as soon as possible, and that you shouldn't go anywhere."

"We know the drill, unfortunately," I say. Paul Lundy goes way back with both of us.

"Where does he think we'd go?"

Essie Sue doesn't share my fondness for Paul—the two of them make up whatever's the opposite of a mutual admiration society. I've been in the middle more times than I can count.

"I hear my name being taken in vain. Got here sooner than I thought."

Paul strides in the front door and kisses me on the cheek.

In my peripheral vision, I see all the police personnel snap to. From what I hear, he's a tough boss.

Essie Sue's not too shaken to raise her eyebrows at the kiss, since she's always been convinced there's something between us. "Did you know Ruby has a new boyfriend?" she says to Paul.

"Jeez, Essie Sue," I say, "could you be any more crass, or is this only your first try? We're in a dead man's house, for openers. Give Paul a chance to do his job."

I haven't spoken to Paul in months, and since we've never been a couple, I certainly don't owe him any updates on my social life. I'll admit we used to flirt a lot, but that's all it was.

Actually, he does seem a bit thrown off by her remark. I've never seen that look on his face before, but he covers it fast.

"What's up?" he says to me. "I understand you two came over because the victim hadn't kept an appointment?"

Essie Sue answers for me. "We didn't have an appointment today. It was yesterday afternoon that he didn't show up, but I haven't been able to reach him by phone, either, so I thought I'd come over."

"And *noodge* him in person," I add.

"Well, it's lucky for him I did, Ruby. He could have been here for days, otherwise."

I wouldn't exactly call it lucky, considering.

"So he could have died within the last twenty-four hours," Paul says.

"I think no more than that, because it looks as though he was preparing some fish to take over to the appointment with Essie Sue when he was killed. And he would have wanted it sliced fresh."

"For the audition."

"Huh?" Paul looks at Essie Sue.

"Don't ask," I say. "She wanted him to show off his wares for an event she's planning at the Temple."

"You'd both better fill me in from the beginning—I'm getting bits and pieces here."

It takes a full hour for Paul's interview—he's thorough. Essie Sue seems to have recovered, but I'm feeling a little shaky toward the end, and he finally picks up on it.

"Sorry, ladies—I know this has been a nerve-racking afternoon." I don't fail to notice the impersonal plural. "I'll call you when I need more."

"Does that mean we can go home?" Essie Sue asks.

"Yes, but call as soon as you get there, and give me the name of the deceased's next of kin—the daughter you said you knew."

"Rose," Essie Sue says. "Do you want me to call her?"

"Definitely not. Just give me her number."

"The rabbi ought to contact her, though. Her child is in his Bar Mitzvah class. I could tell him. . . ."

Paul and I exchange looks. She's obviously dying to get involved.

"I'd really like you to keep quiet for a while until I have a chance to contact the next of kin, Essie Sue."

"Let's go," I say. "Paul needs that unlisted number you have at your house—it'll save him time. And speaking of your house, Essie Sue, how long did you tell Kevin to stay with the kids? Weren't you planning to pick them up at the Temple?"

I can tell she's forgotten all about the boys. If I were in her place, I'd want to forget, too.

"I'm sure the rabbi had sense enough to take them home with him when he didn't hear from me. We'll drop by his apartment."

"Take them home? Are you crazy? That's the last place he'd take them. I wouldn't be surprised if he was parked on your doorstep with them. Isn't Hal there to let them in?"

"No. Hal's playing golf."

"Let's go to the Temple first—maybe he left a message there."

Her mind's still on other things. "I don't care what Lundy thinks," she says. "I'm telling the rabbi as soon as I give them the phone number. He's a professional, too, and he needs to know. You and I can make the condolence call with him."

"Oh, the condolence call—now I get it. Let the woman have a chance to get over the shock, Essie Sue. I wouldn't say you were exactly a close acquaintance—give her family and friends some time to see her first."

"She'll want to see us, Ruby. You and I discovered the body. Wouldn't you, if you were in her place?"

She's got me there. And knowing myself, if I were in her place I'd probably be all over anyone I could corner. Not that I'm ready to tell her that.

"Do us a favor, Essie Sue, and hold off until tomorrow. Then we can talk about it."

Ha—who am I kidding? I'm as curious as she is to talk to the daughter. Meanwhile, Rabbi Kevin must be spitting mad after all these hours. If he's survived.

chapter
7

....

We head straight to the Temple and I run in while
Essie Sue waits in the car—par for the course, even though
we are picking up her relatives. No Kevin. The secretary
has gone home, so the janitor lets me in. He hasn't seen
anyone. I go to the rabbi's study, where under ordinary circumstances, I might assume that either a robbery had taken
place or a tornado had hit. But the debris is only a sign, I
fear, that the Bitman twins' first Hebrew lesson evolved
into disaster. I look in vain for a note, an SOS, or any other
distress signal. All I see is a fleet of paper airplanes covering Kevin's big desk. File drawers are open, and books
from the shelves are stacked up like forts. Who knows—
maybe Kevin built the forts for protection? There's not a
Hebrew primer in sight—he must have given up early.

I check the playschool area, and even the sanctuary,
thinking that Kevin might be rehearsing the boys to kill
some time. Before I leave, I write a quick note in case he
comes back, giving him Essie Sue's cell phone number.

"Not there," I say as I get back in the Lincoln.

"I told you so. He wouldn't keep them at the Temple that

long. We're going to the rabbi's apartment just as I wanted to do in the first place. He's probably feeding them a snack."

Let's hope so—my rabbinical radar is bleeping, and that's not good. Although if anyone's pantry could satisfy Larry's and Lester's preadolescent taste, it would be Kevin's. From what I've seen on previous visits, his food groups all start with D's—Doritos, Domino's, Dunkin' Donuts, Dr Pepper, and Ding Dongs.

We pull up in front of the apartment and ring the bell. No one's there. Then we both remember Kevin's secret hiding place for his door key—under the fake plastic rock at the edge of the doormat. All the delivery carriers and half the apartment complex are also privy to this information, but up to now, no one has broken into the apartment. Not that he knows of, that is—his housekeeping leaves something to be desired. Most of the furnishings inside consist of gym equipment donated by Essie Sue from her now defunct fitness enterprise, the Center for Bodily Movement. We make a quick tour of the two rooms crammed with StairMasters, two kinds of exercise bikes, and a treadmill, and we even check the answering machine. Nothing. No twins. No Kevin.

"What do we do now?" I say.

"My house," she says. "Maybe he found Hal home from golf. I won't be happy about this, though—Hal's not a good supervisor. I told him never to let the boys in the house without me. They can always play outside."

"Oh, so you're saying you'd rather have them tear up our places or the temple offices than touch the House Beautiful when you're not around. Gee, that's a surprise."

"Come on, Ruby. What could they hurt in your house that the three-legged dog hasn't already rampaged? I have *décor*—and you have—*je ne sais quoi?*"

"Try *livable*." I'll take my easy chairs and beautiful golden retriever, Oy Vay, over anything she's got in her McMansion.

We're on our way out Kevin's driveway when Essie Sue's car phone rings. Whatever she hears makes her face turn white—and that's quite a feat under all that blusher.

"What is it?" I ask.

"It's Hal—he's at the golf course. The police tracked him down, looking for me."

"But Lieutenant Lundy knew we were headed to the Temple before we went home—I told him."

"It's not Lundy—it's some other department in the police station. I'm supposed to call the new president of the Temple—Tom Sager—and then go to the station. Remember the number for me—I don't have anything to write on."

We call Tom Sager and are immediately put on hold. Meanwhile, she's tapping her long red-bronze fingernails on the steering wheel—a sure sign she's in stress. Those nails don't get tapped on anything—too much risk of cracking. A broken fingernail in Essie Sue's world is the next worse thing to a bear market. I have to hear the tap, tap, tap for five more minutes before Tom Sager finally gets on the phone. I'm too curious to have to hear this secondhand, so I make her share the earpiece with me, which she's more than willing to do.

"Essie Sue," he says, "I've just sent my lawyer down to the police station—you'd better get down there. They're asking for you."

"Who's asking for me? What's going on, Tom?"

"The rabbi and the boys are being held for questioning."

chapter
8
....

"Ruby, this isn't fair. I told them I'm an important fig-
ure in this town, but it doesn't seem to make any difference."

"Have you seen Paul Lundy yet?"

"No, I asked them to find him, but I don't think they
listened."

We're sitting in the booking section of the police station,
being monitored by a uniformed rookie who appears to be
about ten years old. You know you're getting older when
the cops look younger than your kids. Apparently, Kevin's
not in the Most Dangerous category yet, because the
rookie seems more interested in his copy of *Car and Driver* than in us.

Essie Sue is in another room asserting her authority as
the twins' guardian here in Eternal. My job for the moment
is to reassure Kevin.

"Tom Sager called his lawyer, and he'll be here any
minute, Kevin—I think it's Al Jaffe—he does most of the
legal work for the Temple now."

"Uh-oh. The Jaffe family hasn't liked me since I called
their mother by the wrong name at her funeral. They were

mouthing something at me all during the eulogy, but I thought it was their way of mourning."

"He's a lawyer and a professional," I say. "He's supposed to put aside personal feelings." Right. The last time Al Jaffe put aside personal feelings was at his *bris,* and I'm sure everyone at the circumcision was on his grudge list shortly thereafter. We probably do need Paul. Before I try to call him, though, I want to have a better idea of what's happening—Kevin's told me very little.

"So what did Lester and Larry do that was so delinquent, apart from being their charming selves? And what did you do?"

"I told Essie Sue already—it was all a big mistake. When you didn't come to pick the boys up, I decided to take them home to Essie Sue's, but no one was there. I couldn't think of anything to do with them, and they were begging to go to the mall, so I said we'd go for a little while."

Oy. You'd have to shoot me before I'd let those two loose on the public.

"We had jalapeño cheese tostadas at the Taco House, with pistachio Big Freezes to wash them down. I wanted to leave then, but they insisted on renting some videos. That's where the trouble started. I thought the videos would entertain them if we had to go back to my study and wait for Essie Sue."

"Don't stop now. They tried to slip a video out without registering?"

"They told me I should look at the movie classics section while they checked out the action videos in the back of the main room. It's a big place."

"They slipped out?"

"Not exactly. They said they liked classics, and asked me to pick out two videos for them. They were gone a long time, and when they finally met me back in the classics section, they took my videos and brought them to the desk.

I was going to sign them out under my membership. The boys went into the mall corridor to wait for me. That's when I got detained."

I'm afraid to ask, but he plunges on.

"When the computer screen registered the films I was renting, it showed *Annie Get Your Gun* and *High Noon.* But then my jacket beeped. The twins had slipped *Darla Does Dallas,* and *A Tour of Nevada Ranch Houses* into my coat pockets. The clerk called the manager."

"And of course the boys didn't say they put them in your pockets?"

"Well, in all fairness, when we brought Larry and Lester back in, they did tell the clerk that we all liked cowboy movies. I think they were trying to help me out."

"Uh-huh. And the manager bought this just like you did?"

"I don't think he was too impressed with any of it. He said he was going to call the police."

"They took you in a squad car?"

"No, they took us to this detention place at Mall Security, and *they* took us to the police."

"Why? Couldn't you straighten it out there?"

"I stood up to them. I insisted that they call the Eternal Ministerial Association—I was just elected secretary, it's an ecumenical group, and it's very prestigious; and that I wasn't a thief."

"Yeah, and how did that go over?"

"That's when they called the cops."

"What's up, Rabbi?" This from Al Jaffe, who's just walked up to us—he's a casual kind of guy, with a friendly grin for every occasion. I can see right away that he's thrilled to be here—the grin's a bit lopsided around the edges, and shows signs of collapsing altogether.

"I just told the whole story to Ruby—she'll tell you. I'm tired."

"Who am I? Lawyer to your lawyer? Nothing doing." I'm thinking that after calling Al's mother by the wrong name throughout her eulogy, Kevin could manage to be a bit more gracious in his hour of need, but that's his problem.

"He's all yours," I say to Al. I can be more helpful finding Paul than trying to explain Kevin to his lawyer.

Although I could reach Paul through the reception desk, I'm trying his cell phone first. No answer, so I start toward the front office, when I hear Essie Sue's dulcet tones, making life miserable for some lucky police officer.

"Are you finished questioning these little boys? You saw the Temple lawyer come in, so surely you'll get enough information from him to release Rabbi Kapstein immediately."

"Lady, just one of these *little* boys could throw me without half trying. I didn't think they were gonna wither like daisies on the vine if we encouraged them to cooperate. They say they thought they were cowboy movies and slipped them into the rabbi's pockets because his hands were full."

"Then you can take that to the bank, Officer. My little cousins are in town for religious training."

I'm about to turn the other way and run, when Paul walks in the door.

"What're you doing here, Ruby?"

"Nice seeing you, too. Kevin's gotten himself into a mess, and now that you're back, I'm feeling safe enough to take off."

"Nothing doing, Ruby—I see Mrs. Margolis over there. I'm not getting involved until you fill me in."

"Gotta run."

"You give me ten minutes, I'll give you ten. Or you can leave now, and not hear the latest on what we found this afternoon after you left the Guenther house. There's been a new development."

chapter 9

....

Paul spreads out a paper towel on his desk and sprin-
kles salted peanuts on it—this is big hospitality at the station house.

"Diet or regular?"

"Diet."

He's already popped the top of a Diet Coke and hands it
to me.

"So why do you ask, if you know I want Diet?"

"Just to pull your chain, Ruby. What's up with Essie Sue
and the rabbi?"

I give him a quick fill-in and he snorts. "I really need
this on top of a murder investigation, Ruby."

"So can you at least help me get them out of here?"

"Let's see what's going on." He heads toward the front
desk.

"Whoa," I say, "sit back down. You promised to tell me
the new development—how could anything happen that
fast? It hasn't been that long since we left you at Herman's."

"I asked one of the uniforms to look around. She found a

carbon copy of a letter he'd written last week to the distributor who supplied lox for his catering business."

"A computer copy?"

"No, the old-fashioned kind—typed on a vintage Underwood. The copy was onionskin—crinkled almost beyond recognition, but he hadn't thrown it away. It was lying right on the desktop."

"I told you when you interviewed us at the house that he was having problems with those people. He even spoke to Ed about it when we ran into him at the bakery once. He wanted Ed to do an exposé for his newspaper."

"You didn't say that earlier."

"I forgot about it—sorry. Ed works for the daily in San Antonio, and the distributor has business there, too. They're the same people our guy Rocko represents, and we aren't happy with them, either."

I get a funny look from Paul—he's either surprised that I forgot, or he's thinking I didn't want to talk about Ed. I'm not sure which it is—maybe a little of both.

"What happened with the story?"

"Ed looked into it, but Herman wasn't willing to be interviewed for the piece—at least, by name—and the editors nixed it. So what did he say in the letter you found?"

"He was angry. He told them that he knew the business well enough to be sure they were jacking up prices way beyond market, and they were taking advantage of small buyers who only knew that costs had risen in general. He mentioned wholesalers he knew in New York and Los Angeles and federal regulations concerning contamination. He didn't threaten specifically to go to the authorities, but it was implied."

"*Oy.* I wonder if the man knew who he was dealing with."

"Apparently he did but was furious enough not to care."

"What are you going to do now?"

"I'm not sure. At any rate, I can't sit here and kill time

with you. Let's go clean out the place—my men have more important things to do."

"Your men?"

"And women. Don't call the gender cops on me."

"Unfortunately, you are the cops. Are you going to rescue Kevin? I can just see Essie Sue's troops in blue armbands yelling *Free Rabbi Kapstein*."

That gets a rare laugh out of him. He has a cute smile.

"Hey, Kevin," I yell as I catch sight of him trying to outtalk his lawyer. "You're gonna be sprung."

Several official heads go up at my announcement, looking relieved—including Al Jaffe's.

"They'd better," Kevin says, "unless they're ready for a lawsuit for false arrest."

At this point, Al grabs Kevin, puts his hand on top of his head, and shoves him down into a chair. "You know about gift horses, Rabbi? Keep quiet."

I follow Paul into the room where Essie Sue's holding forth on behalf of her boys. The subjects of all this commotion are slightly cowed—either that, or they're aching from the Taco House tostadas. Their arms are folded on the table, making a resting place for their heads. To look at them, you'd never know they were capable of generating a tornado. Obviously, the intense questioning on the part of the Eternal police has done them in.

"Let me talk to these kids," Paul says.

Essie Sue keeps at it. "Don't they need their lawyer?"

"Don't push it, Essie Sue," I say before Paul busts a gut. "Come out in the hall with me. The boys will be fine—it's Kevin you need to calm down."

I hear him before I see him.

"I want my one phone call."

"Uh, Kevin, don't you think it's a little late for that? You already have a lawyer here."

"Yeah, but someone else called him. One of the officers

called the Temple president for me, and he called the lawyer. I haven't called anyone."

"Rabbi," Essie Sue says, "who are you calling?"

"The *Eternal Ear.* This is a front-page story, Essie Sue. One of the area's leading clergymen has been defamed. I think we should get a photographer down here."

For once I don't have to do anything. I'll say this for Essie Sue—she knows a disaster in the making; she's unstoppable when her PR buttons are pushed.

"Are you crazy, Rabbi? This is something you should hope everyone forgets, not publicizes."

"But, Essie Sue, this story has everything I need to vindicate me—police brutality, your grand-cousins . . ."

I'm transfixed. "And you want this in the papers?"

"But I'm not guilty. I'm a spiritual force in this community, and I want my day in court. I already have the lawyer."

The color is draining from Al Jaffe's face, and that boyish grin has morphed into something out of a horror movie. He looks at Essie Sue.

"This I'm doing for nothing?"

"You've gone beyond the call of duty, Al. I'll take it from here."

Essie Sue takes Kevin aside. I don't know what she's telling him, but I'll bet the words *Darla Does Dallas* and *Rabbinical Placement Committee* feature prominently.

chapter
10

....

"By the way, what are you wearing?"

I'm sitting in the middle of my bed at almost midnight, on the phone with Ed. On one side of me is Oy Vay watching muted TV, and on the other side is a pile of *New York Times Book Review*s I'm trying to reduce by half.

"I'm wearing a pair of shorts and a tank top," I say. "Is that what you were fantasizing?"

"It'll do. Reminds me of the first time I saw you on the ship last year."

"In that case, I should add the orange life jacket."

"That's okay long distance, but when we get together, you can skip it. Doesn't do a thing for you."

"Now that you bring it up, when *are* we getting together?"

"Hey, Ruby, I'm not the only one hard to get—you've been unavailable a lot, too. Remember week before last when you were rescuing that client from being eaten by his hard drive?"

"No, his data was being eaten by his hard drive—it was turning the letters into little hollow squares whenever he tried to save them. And I wasn't complaining that it was your fault we hadn't been together—where did you get that from?"

"I thought you were insinuating. Bottom line is that it was you who told *me* not to come."

"And then I didn't hear from you for days after."

"I was pissed."

"So I gathered. But I wasn't supposed to mind when you didn't show up the weekend before, and only remembered to call me two hours after you had said you'd be here?"

"That was an emergency assignment—you know that."

"But you do have a cell phone."

"I used it as soon as I remembered. Is this fun, Ruby?"

"No. I'm sorry."

"Me, too. I didn't want to start bickering, because you're not going to like this."

"This what?"

"This other thing. I can't come up for the next two weekends, either. The guy I'm working with for the Mexico story wants a preliminary meeting in Mazatlán to get some things worked out, and the weekend after that is the only time my sister has free to talk about her divorce. You knew about that one, right?"

"No, I didn't know that was a weekend. And pardon me, did you say you *had* to go to Mazatlán? Poor baby."

"I wish you could go with me, but you know that's not possible."

"Yeah, yeah. So can we plan something?"

"Sure."

"Ed, do you realize we're always planning something? Except that it never works out. Plans are cheap."

"It's not just me, Ruby."

"I know, but I can't deal with another set of plans tonight."

"So are you hanging up?"

"Do you want me to?"

"No. Let's change the subject."

"We always do. Strike that—it's not fair. I'm the one who couldn't deal with it tonight. But I do have something I have to ask you."

I'm grabbing the cordless phone and running downstairs for a Diet Coke while I'm talking. I know it could keep me up—I don't buy the decaffeinated kind—but I get antsy lately every time I argue with Ed, and the drink will keep me from eating. I hope.

"Whatever you have to ask me sounds serious, Ruby."

"Hold on a minute—I'm back upstairs and trying to get some of this junk off my bed."

"The junk doesn't include Oy Vay, I hope."

"Ha—she's so secure she wouldn't even be insulted. No, she's a fixture. This is what I wanted to say. I was so upset last night when I told you about my hellish afternoon that I forgot to tell you Paul wanted to question you this weekend when you came up. About Herman's conversations with you."

"But Paul neglected to tell me?"

"Give him a break, honey—I had thought you'd be up this weekend for sure. The appointment wasn't carved in stone."

"Tell Paul he can call me himself—it's not exactly professional to use you as a go-between."

"Look, Ed, it's not that formal—I'm sure he was going to call you, and *will* still call you when he finds out you won't be here. But at least satisfy my curiosity. What kind of exposé did Herman want you to do?"

"He wanted me to investigate the entire distribution system—salmon from the Pacific Northwest as well as outlets in the East. People with gripes usually think the paper has unlimited funding for this sort of thing. But since he wanted to be kept out of it, the story didn't have much punch."

"Did you find out anything about his personal life?"

"Herman was an interesting character. He talked about

his background as a lox slicer in New York, and he had an interesting youth in northern Europe during the Hitler era. But I doubt the inquiry would have materialized without his active participation."

"He was a bit hotheaded, don't you think, Ed? I wonder if he ever lost his temper with specific individuals and told them he was planning to publicly expose them?"

"Let's say I wouldn't be shocked to hear it, although that's a dangerous game. For everybody."

"Well, I sure hope he didn't. I'm sleepy, honey—it's past midnight. Call me tomorrow?"

"Are you angry?"

"Not if you aren't."

I lay awake for a long time after we finally hung up. Long distance is a bitch.

chapter
11

·····················

Herman was an endearing man, and his daughter Rose is even more so. She insists on serving me iced tea and cookies, even though she's clearly a basket case and is barely holding herself together. I've had experience with sudden death—that call from the police that changes your life—and I can only imagine how overwhelming it was for her to hear that her father had been taken from her in such a violent way.

Conversation is difficult—even my clergy wife skills can't compensate for the fact that we're strangers to each other, and I'm relieved when her preteen daughter comes home from school.

"This is Jackie, Ruby—she's twelve."

Apparently the family consists of Jackie, an older brother at college, and Rose's husband, Ray, who's a printer.

It's hard for me to believe that this tall, poised young woman is Larry and Lester's age and about to be Bat Mitzvahed in the same class. Gender aside, it's the Godzilla twins meeting Fay Wray. I'm assuming she hasn't made their acquaintance yet. She has long straight brown hair I'd have killed for—the kind that looks good no matter what you do with it. She's brushed it behind her ears, letting it fall halfway down her back.

"Jackie's almost as tall as I am," Rose says. "She takes after her father, while I was the runt of the litter—small, like her grandpa." Both she and Jackie tear up and lean against each other at the reference to Herman.

I tell her about the twins who'll be in her class, and she politely feigns interest—or who knows, maybe she really *is* curious, and wondering if they're cute. Needless to say, I'm grateful they're only an abstraction at this point. When she leaves the room, I'm happy to notice that her appearance seems to have broken the ice between Rose and me. Rose seems more relaxed, and I feel I can safely ask some questions about her father.

"I noticed some old photos of rural landscapes in his house, along with pictures of your family."

She seems distracted. "They were in his living room." Then she remembers why I would have been there.

"He appeared to be sleeping when I saw him at the table," I say. "I truly believe it happened so fast he had no warning and no suffering."

"I'm so relieved to hear that. No one said so."

I tell her that the police who are busy investigating a crime scene don't always prioritize the things loved ones want to hear. When my own husband, Stu, was the victim of a hit-and-run, I was told about it in a way I wouldn't wish on anyone, but I keep that to myself. She's involved in her grief, not mine.

To my surprise and satisfaction, Rose picks up on my remarks about Herman's photos. The past is probably a lot more comforting to her than the present.

"My father was born in a rural area north of Berlin, between the World Wars. When he was a teenager, he went to live in Scandinavia—that's where he first learned a trade. He worked in a smokehouse processing fish."

"How did he happen to leave home?"

"Some of my father's schoolmates had joined the Hitler Youth. He always had a nose for trouble, and when he saw firsthand the attraction the Nazis had for those who had been his friends, he was far more ready to take the party seriously than others he knew. Even his own family thought he was being overly suspicious."

"He didn't tell you more?"

"No, he said nothing to us about that time in his life. Ten years later, he was already living in the United States, where he met and married my mother. When she told me he'd shared very little with her, either, I decided it was pointless to ask."

"I admire your restraint," I say. "I'd probably have kept burrowing."

"My father was a loving man, and thinking back saddened him. He did tell us that he was lucky he left Germany when he did and missed the concentration camps, but that's all he'd say. He always got such a look in his eyes when I prodded him. Even as a youngster, I really didn't want to be responsible for that look."

Jackie comes back into the room with a question about the memorial service for her grandfather, and I know it's time to go. I offer to help out during the difficult week to come, and Rose says she might take me up on it, especially when she has to clean out her father's house. I sense there's not a huge support system here, and maybe I can be useful. Not to mention my curiosity about what's in that house that the police might have missed.

chapter
12

· ·

E-mail from: Ruby
To: Nan
Subject: *Our Less Than Tropical Vacation*

Tell me again why you're going to Alaska in November? That's not exactly tourist season, is it—even for conferences? I've heard that many of the sights are closed down or frozen in from November through the winter season. I've got to be honest with you—I wasn't paying close attention when you mentioned this before. I didn't really think I'd be able to join you, but now I'm listening.

· ·

E-mail from: Nan
To: Ruby
Subject: *Alaska*

Before I regale you with winter scenes to die for, I'm curious. Why are you listening *now*? It couldn't have anything to do with your love life, could it? Just a guess.

••

E-mail from: Ruby
To: Nan
Subject: *Alaska*

Guess, my foot. I hate it when you sneak inside my mind, but yes, it does kind of have something to do with Ed. I knew he was going to Mexico for that big assignment later in the year, but I didn't know it was Mazatlán—I thought it was some place I *wouldn't* want to visit! We're getting along okay—just having a lot of trouble getting our schedules in sync. I was depressed about our communication in general and about his being away for so long in particular, and then I remembered your offer. I don't see why I can't do something really fun, too.

••

E-mail from: Nan
To: Ruby
Subject: *Your Boyfriend*

Thanks for the explanation. My only wish is to serve. Somehow I knew this wasn't about Alaska, and I'm oh so thrilled to give you a chance to show Ed he isn't the only one who can have an adventure. Just for once, I'd like not to be your best friend and just pretend I'm a lovely acquaintance whose company is your first priority. But as they so tritely say, "What are best friends for?"

Now for why we're going to Alaska in the wintertime. This is a committee dealing with a Forest Service matter that has to be resolved in the month of November. My way will be paid. You can stay in the room for no cost. It'll be a cheap way for you to come along, if you can swing the plane ticket. One hearing is in Anchorage, and the other, a few days later, is in Fairbanks, which isn't too far from Denali. I hear it's a hoot taking the local trains in winter—they disconnect all the tourist cars and just use one engine.

You keep me posted about the murdered lox slicer, and I'll keep you posted about the trip.

••

E-mail from: Ruby
To: Nan
Subject: *Red-faced*

I'm sorry I'm such a lousy friend—too bad we're joined at the hip and you're stuck with me for life. I do want to see you—you know that, and I know we'll have a ball if I do come along. I'll be happy to be the schlep-along and get in on a cheap trip, too, although I can't really afford even this much.

This does have something to do with Ed—I can't deny that—at least that was an impetus to get me moving on your offer. And I might as well confess that I'm also planning to check out a fish distributor Herman was dealing with in Kodiak or Seattle. So I have three things pushing me now—YOU, the Ed stuff, and some leads on the killing.

Paul is pursuing other angles on Herman's murder having to do with written accusations Herman made against his distributors. I'm trying to look into other aspects of his life, and his daughter's letting me help pack up his belongings this week. Who knows? Maybe we'll get lucky.

chapter
13

....

Essie Sue's Lincoln pulls up to the entrance circle of Austin's newest golf and country club, and three attendants spring to attention. I had no idea she was such a good tipper. Either that, or the level of service has increased dramatically in our state capital up the highway from Eternal, something I seriously doubt.

"Looks as though these guys know you," I say.

"I gave them good reason to. They don't have many ethnic representatives in this club, and I didn't want anyone thinking Hal and I are cheap."

She usually *is* cheap, but I suppose this isn't the place to point that out. I'm on my good behavior for lunch, because I have an agenda. In fact, we're each hoping to get something from the other today, so we're both being extra nice. That needn't mean, though, that I'm going to censor myself altogether. There are some things I can't let go by.

"Ethnic representatives? Is that where they do ethnic cleansing and then start all over again with better examples?"

"No, this is a new club, Ruby, and it's very inclusive. We

only got in because we're from Eternal, not Austin, so it gave the club a chance to include a Jewish family from another town. For a while we were running neck and neck with the Kantor family—he's a much better golfer than Hal—but I finessed Sara Kantor."

I'm almost afraid to ask.

"How?"

"Because I pointed out to my friend on the applications committee that I was still vice president of Temple Rita. That way, they're able to honor the whole congregation I represent, whereas with the Kantors, it's only golf."

"It *is* a golf club, isn't it?"

"A golf club with social responsibility, Ruby. Soon, I'm going to ask them to give the rabbi a clergy membership."

I can't deal with Essie Sue's warped version of social action today, even more so when it's interspersed with visions of Kevin in plaid golf shorts.

"Are you sure I won't be too much for them as your luncheon guest, Essie Sue? Maybe someone's already bringing another minority. I wouldn't want to tip the balance in the wrong direction, especially since we're planning a Bar Mitzvah. Aren't you afraid that's subversive?"

"Enough, Ruby. I want you to put an ecumenical smile on your face and enjoy yourself, you hear? This is supposed to be a treat."

No, not a treat—just a chance to probe a bit on the subject of Essie Sue's relationship, however superficial, with Herman Guenther. In return, I'm indulging her obsession with the Bar Mitzvah plans.

The place is packed—apparently there *are* still ladies who lunch. I expected an older crowd, but I also see tables full of soccer moms politely scarfing down the chicken salad. The men must be in the bar or on the golf course—this is definitely female territory.

"Did you notice the pink carnations on the table, Ruby? Not fake, either. This is an A-1 establishment."

"I wouldn't expect anything less from you, Essie Sue."

"Eat all you want. We have to spend a certain amount in the dining room each month, and we were out of town for part of the time."

Well, that explains why I'm invited for a meal, anyway. Essie Sue usually doesn't waste valuable social time on me, apart from Temple events. Now we have to eat the quota.

The waiter comes and I order a frozen margarita.

"At lunch? I don't think so, Ruby."

"Look around, Essie Sue."

The waiter comes to my rescue by pointing out that the frozen margarita is very popular today. His input obviously seals the deal, because she resigns herself to joining me.

"I'll have a white wine, then."

"It's not the money, Ruby—your choice simply didn't seem in good taste."

This from the woman who complimented the pink and blue tacos on our recent cruise to St. Thomas.

"I want you to order an appetizer and dessert as well as an entrée today—I don't want to have to drive all the way back to use up the monthly fee."

I knew she'd come through in the class department.

"If we can't eat it all, Essie Sue, I'm sure they'll provide doggie bags."

Her gasp makes me decide to take it back.

"Just kidding. Oy Vay doesn't like country club food."

Our drinks are served, and we settle on stuffed mushrooms for openers, with chicken salad to follow. I have my eye on Key lime pie for later.

I take advantage of the fact that we're surrounded by people she wants to impress. She's malleable. If I can get my part of this meeting done before lunch arrives, then I'll be prepared to deal with the Bar Mitzvah details over dessert. I do, however, borrow the topic in order to get things started.

"It'll be sad not having Herman at his granddaughter's Bat Mitzvah—we'll have to make it extra comfortable for her without him."

"Well, I certainly hope it won't be sad—Larry and Lester will deserve a celebration after all their hard work. Since it's a combined ceremony, she'll have to be happy, too, for their sakes."

"And they might have to be a bit compassionate for hers?"

As if they know the concept.

"I'm not working all year for a funereal atmosphere, Ruby—forget that. Besides, Herman Guenther wasn't exactly making my life easier."

"I thought you were raving about him."

"That was before he died. Now that he's gone, I'm remembering how stubborn he was."

I can see where the twins get their compassion.

"There's a lot you don't know, Ruby."

Now we're getting someplace. If I'm interested, she'll change the subject, so I try to look bored, but not too bored. This isn't easy, but the food comes and I play with my fork without looking up. They make a mean margarita here, but the mushrooms are as bland as the crowd.

"Don't you want to know how stubborn Herman was?"

"Sure."

"I gave him some really nice publicity for his catering business, and how did he thank me? He yelled at me—I was terribly hurt."

I've been the recipient of some of those favors that could provoke curses, but I hold back.

"U'mm—that's too bad. What did he yell about?"

"It happened at the wedding I told you about—months ago when Brother Copeland's son married the Newman girl. I had the wedding photographer take some telephoto shots of the kitchen preparations, and Herman was filmed putting the finishing touches on a lox platter. I know you remember that informative article about the wedding that I wrote for the *Eternal Ear*, yes?"

"Sure," I lie.

"Well, I included that shot of Herman, and since he wasn't a reader of the *Ear*, he didn't learn about it until someone mentioned it to him months later. He had a fit. He told me he had no knowledge that the photo had been taken, and that I should have asked for his permission. I pointed out to him that I had insisted that it be shot from the social hall instead of the kitchen so that he and his staff wouldn't be disturbed in their work."

"And he didn't go for that?"

"No, he didn't even appreciate my thoughtfulness. He was so unappreciative that I didn't dare tell him about the other thing I'd done right after the wedding."

Uh-oh. "And what was that?"

"I was so encouraged by the excellent newspaper article I wrote that I expanded it for a Jewish Web site. I asked Herman's daughter, Rose, for a photo of him as a young man, and I told her it would be a surprise for him. You should see the Web site—the photos scanned beautifully."

"This was after you knew how upset he was?"

"Of course not—it was before."

"Why did you want an early photo?"

"Because I told the Jewish Web site master, or whatever he's called, that Herman had learned about the fish-smoking process when he was a young man in Scandinavia. The master thought it was interesting and encouraged me."

"I still don't get why you did this on your own, without interviewing Herman."

"I told you, I wanted to surprise him."

"Come on, Essie Sue—you hardly knew the man personally."

"Well, the truth is that I knew Herman was one of those

opinionated people, and I didn't want him controlling what I wrote, after I got such encouragement from the Web site about my work."

When it comes to control freaks, it takes one to know one. I guess she'd met her match.

My eye's still on the Key lime pie zipping by our table, and we finally get around to ordering it with black coffee. Yum.

"And then, of course," she says, "I also didn't want Herman's part of the story taking over my Web site article. It didn't feel right to me when the master asked me for another photo of Herman—I complied, but I felt as if the piece was slipping away from me."

"And what Herman didn't know wouldn't hurt him?"

"You could say that."

And I do.

chapter
14

·······················

Rose hardly remembers the photo she gave Essie Sue when I ask her about it. We're both exhausted from lugging around heavy cardboard cartons from Herman's attic. Even if we weren't worn out from the physical labor, the sheer emotional load that hangs in the air when a deceased person's belongings are collected is overwhelming. And if that person is a loved one, it's worse, so I know how hard this is for Rose. Not to mention the fact that this wasn't a natural death.

We make small talk about the memorial service a few days ago, but there's not much to say. Most of Eternal didn't know Herman, and the crowd gathered at the cemetery was a small one. Fortunately for all of us, Kevin wasn't asked to do a eulogy, just a brief graveside service. Kevin's handling of death is not what you'd exactly call professional. I feel for the faculty member at the seminary who had to *teach* him the subtleties of human nature in crisis, when the reality is that you can't school someone in common sense. He veers from being totally tongue-tied to spouting meaningless words. And body language, he doesn't know from.

There are so many times when just a look will make a mourner feel understood, but if you don't have that touch, you can't give it, and all the graduate schooling in the world won't help. Even with the brief service, Kevin seems to have scored a minus one with Rose.

"I was surprised, Ruby, that the rabbi had so little to say to us personally after the service. Or before, for that matter. I know we aren't old standbys of the congregation, but we have known him for a while. It was as if we were total strangers to him."

What can I say? That Kevin probably froze in his tracks? That he can read the right words from a book, but can't wing it between the lines?

"My guess is that he both knows and likes you, Rose, but that he's uncomfortable with certain parts of the job."

"But that *is* his job, isn't it?"

I think I'm making things worse by trying to explain him. Lucky for me, she abandons the emotional for the physical, and gets back to work.

When Rose opens some of her father's bureau drawers, I can see her visibly recoil. I know it's because of the ordinary, everyday odors that still linger in a person's home after death. Just when you think you've got a grip on yourself, you pull open a long-closed drawer and the smell of the neatly folded clothes brings back the ghost as if the person were still standing there. I've been through it.

I go into Herman's kitchen to make us two mugs of oolong tea—no tea bags here, either, I notice with satisfaction. I don't know about Rose, but I need the strong brew today. It's not easy to walk into this kitchen and look out on the back porch where Herman was stabbed. The whole house gives me the creeps, actually, but helping out is the least I can do. I keep reminding myself that it's got to be twice as hard for Rose. We'd ordinarily take our break on the back porch, I'm sure, but we're both studiously avoiding that end of the house except for quick runs like this one for the tea. We're concentrating instead on the boxes from the attic, and on a few of the overstuffed bookshelves where papers have been stored.

Earlier this morning we ran into some yellowed papers in Yiddish—I think they're personal correspondence or journals of some kind. Rose was wondering if they might not be letters from Herman's family, written before the war. Rose has a relative in town who reads Yiddish as well as anyone else we can come up with in the Jewish netherworld of Eternal, Texas, and she's planning to take them over to the man's house for translation. Our other choice was Essie Sue, who also reads Yiddish, but a quick look between us put an end to that option.

"I think I'd be happier keeping Essie Sue out of my family's business," Rose says. "I know she means well, but—"

"You don't have to explain to me," I say. "And unfortunately, she doesn't always mean well."

"My father said she really pressured him for discounts."

"*Pressure* would be her middle name if *discount* hadn't gotten there first, Rose. I gather they had many words about the lox prices."

"It was the *way* she pressured him that got to me. She told him he was unknown here, and that he should be paying her for introducing him to congregants who might use him. I think she was even hoping he'd do the job for free."

"That sounds like Essie Sue. And after working in New York, I'm sure Herman was bowled over by the chance to make a name for himself in Eternal, Texas."

At least this brings a little smile to her face. "He liked being here, Ruby, but for him, this was just a chance to earn some money in retirement."

"You're remarkably restrained," I say. "What did you think when she asked you to get that old photo for her?"

I've been wondering how to bring this up again as part of the conversation, but I can't think of any subtle way to do it.

"Well, by the time she asked me, the wedding was over and everyone, including Essie Sue, seemed pleased with my dad's catering. I also knew by then that her cousins would be celebrating their Bar Mitzvahs along with my daughter. I suppose I was feeling expansive and wanting to be a part of things. She said she had some photos for him, and wanted to make a little album as a surprise, including his picture as a young man. I had a favorite that my mother had given me long ago—I'm not sure my dad even knew I had it."

"Essie Sue can be quite convincing, can't she?"

"Oh yes. Have you seen the album? I haven't."

I suddenly remember that Rose has no idea about Herman's photo being broadcast on the Web, and since I haven't even told Paul yet, I decide not to complicate things.

"No, but Essie Sue doesn't always follow up. Does she still have the photo?"

"Oh no, she just borrowed it to scan into her computer, and gave it back to me. That's why I'd forgotten about it."

I change the subject.

"I'm sorry your father was unfortunate enough to come smack up against Essie Sue's bargain-basement mentality, but I did hear nothing but raves about the food at the wedding."

"The family was happy it went well. And the truth was that my dad *did* think the fish prices were exorbitant—I told the police I'd be on the lookout for an answer to the letters he wrote to those suppliers."

I suggest that we abandon the cardboard boxes for a while and concentrate on the bookshelves—it's much more likely that Herman would have stored the recent correspondence within his reach. He doesn't have a desk per se, so we can't search drawers—his typewriter was on a card table. He apparently used whatever space was at hand as his writing area.

"I think I've found something," Rose says. She grabs a bunch of papers, which at least don't look a zillion years old. The pile is a mess, but it's a fresh mess. We search through a bunch of recent bills and find the letter we're looking for, stuck between the pages of a medical bill. I'm surprised the police search didn't turn it up.

"It's from Acme Jobbers of Seattle and Kodiak, and it's written to Herman:

> *Dear Mr. Guenther:*
> *We recently received a disturbing letter from you, concerning our distributing system in the state of Texas, operated by Mr. Rocko Pearl. In that letter you allege that our wholesale prices are falsely inflated, that we are fraudulently controlling supplies of smoked salmon, and that we have made threats to close down your private catering business.*
>
> *As you can imagine, we take such charges extremely seriously and assume you are prepared to back up these slanderous assaults upon our good name. We have turned the matter over to our attorneys for further action, and shall contact you in the very near future.*

"So what do you think, Ruby?"

"I think your father made some pretty tough charges," I say. "We both read the letter he wrote these people. I hope he knew who he was dealing with."

"Still," Rose says, "the answer doesn't seem all that threatening—they're responding just as any organization would under the circumstances. My dad had a hot temper—

I told him to keep it under control, but of course he never listened."

"Yeah, I guess mentioning legal action *is* rather standard. I'd like to know more about them, though. I have a friend who lives in Seattle—maybe she could ask around, or at least drive by the place of business."

I picked up my cell phone and called Nan, hoping she's not at lunch. She's not.

"Hey, it's me. Are you too busy to talk?"

"No, just hungry, but what else is new? I get hungry when I'm bored, and the brief I'm working on isn't what one could call stimulating, unless the intricacies of trust disbursement turn you on."

"Not this afternoon—or morning for you. I'm sure you wouldn't have any reason to know anything about a company called Acme Jobbers, but I just thought I'd try. It's the outfit I was going to look up on our vacation, and as I might have mentioned, they have plants or offices in Seattle and Kodiak."

I give her the address and she tells me it's downtown—no surprise, I guess. The neighborhood is near the Market. Certainly that's the place for anything having to do with fish.

"Can you contact some consumer organizations and find out if this company is kosher? I don't mean kosher kosher, I just mean legitimate." Even as I speak, I realize that this is going to be futile. I already know they're legit enough to have done business with us and with Herman, so I'm sure they do what they say they do on the letterhead. Anything else will take a lot more investigation than Nan can provide.

"I'll see what I can do. My boss uses a private investigator I've come to know. Maybe he'll do me a favor and make a call or two."

"Great." I fill her in a bit and tell her I'm with Rose.

"Give her my condolences, okay? I'm glad to try and help."

We hang up and I explain to Rose about our trip-to-be.

"November?" she says. "That's so far away."

"You're right. This whole thing will be cleared up by then."

Let's hope so.

chapter
15

....

It's too hot to be cooking, but I'm motivated—to a point. Ed arrives in a few hours, and I'm making his favorite chili recipe. He brought it home from the Hatch Chili Festival in Hatch, New Mexico, and we tried it together once at his house in San Antonio. Of course, then I had his help, and now I'm on my own, which is not a good thing when it comes to the culinary arts. I'm stirring and hoping that the heat from the three kinds of chilies will numb any flaws that might show up due to my total lack of interest in this procedure. My mind is not on the eats, but on us.

Our relation*ship* is definitely in the wrong port. I'm not sure why, but the seas have been rocky ever since the Caribbean cruise from hell wrapped up. Maybe it's the ethereal nature of shipboard romances, although one would think that having faced possible death with one's beloved might provide all the grounding necessary.

The trouble between Ed and me began almost as soon as I got back to Eternal from St. Thomas. True, we had a few great phone conversations and hot and heavy e-mail exchanges before we were able to visit in person, but they didn't quite carry us through. After that long buildup, we admittedly didn't do a lot of talking when we finally got together in San Antonio. From that perspective it was exhilarating, but I came home realizing I didn't know him much better than I had before, and wasn't likely to do so unless I pushed it.

If I'd thought Ed was taciturn onboard ship, he was even more so later. We had our usual wordplay going, but that's just the one-upsmanship we indulge in when we're avoiding real conversation. I'm usually good at pinpointing problems, but in this case I can't decide whether we have nothing of substance to say to each other or if we're each afraid to get beyond the superficial. I suspect it's the latter, and that we've both made such good adjustments to being on our own that we're steering away from letting another person in. I mean really in—the kind of in that breaks boundaries and is scary as hell.

Oy Vay is going crazy from the piquant aroma of meat and spices.

"Hey, this ain't bad," I tell her with a touch of surprise. It really isn't bad. I've gone all out and made a peach cobbler, too—this one a Central Texas specialty featuring just-picked Sentinels—peaches from Fredericksburg in the Hill Country west of Eternal. I learned years ago that you really can't ruin cobbler. Unlike pies and cakes, which have to be babied, rolled out, or at least carefully measured to work, cobbler can't fall or fail. The dough doesn't shine on its own, but simply serves to make the fruit taste better.

I suppose it's only a coincidence that I'm not serving salmon or some entrée that has to be timed. This whole meal can be postponed for as much time as necessary, if food isn't on our minds yet. Of course, we can't leave Oy Vay alone in the kitchen.

The dinner has already been put on hold once today for reasons having nothing to do with romance. Ed was delayed, and instead of pulling up in my driveway earlier, he called to tell me he wouldn't be leaving San Antonio for a couple of hours. I look at my clock and realize those two hours have passed. Aside from the usual tingle I always get from his impending visits, I'm also dealing with that edge our recent skirmishes have produced. I tell myself I don't care, but working half the afternoon on homemade chili and cobbler says otherwise, and I know it.

Oy Vay's excited bark tells me he's here—they've bonded.

Ed bangs the back screen door on his way into the kitchen, and swings me around, stirring spoon and all. He still smells wonderful, and I'm also still crazy about that lock of hair that I love to push out of the way when I touch his face.

"Glad to see you, babe. Sorry I am late."

He gives me a kiss on the lips and snatches the spoon.

"Hey, I think I got shortchanged on that hello in favor of the chili."

"Can't I be starved for you both at the same time?"

"I guess you did grab me first. Barely."

"As long as you're only jealous of a chili spoon, I guess I'm not in too much trouble, huh?"

"Not too much. It is late, and I bet you're ravenous."

"I was so hungry I was tempted to get a bag of chips on the way up, but I restrained myself."

"You're certainly in a good mood for a hungry man. Wanna have dinner now?"

"Let's relax for a few minutes. Lemme go wash up and maybe you can turn the fire down."

Or up. That one's so obvious we leave it alone, but not without a quiet guffaw.

I'm hungry myself, but I assess my priorities and take a bottle of Pinot Grigiot and two glasses upstairs.

It would take an awful lot to counteract bed, a piping hot meal with all the fixings, two good wines, dessert, and Kenya coffee, but we manage to do it and start sparring before midnight. I've brought up my trip to Alaska over anisette in the living room, and Ed's suddenly become a lump.

"You're saying nothing again, Ed. You know how much I hate that."

"What do you want me to say? You've planned this Alaska thing exactly when I'm coming back from the Mexico assignment. I'll hardly get to see you."

He hardly gets to see me anyway, but I'm trying to keep my cool. And there is the fact that I wanted to go along with Nan partly because it would give me something to look forward to during the time Ed was away.

"Do you think my timing was deliberate, Ed? I'd obviously have chosen to go while you were gone. But this trip is built around Nan's conference, and that's why I'm getting the free room. You know that."

"So do you have to go? After all, it's her conference. You could plan a vacation some other time—not after we've been apart for months."

"I can't believe we're having this conversation. I'm going for two weeks. I'd think you'd be glad for me."

"My trip's for business—yours is for pleasure. I was hoping we could have our vacations together."

"Are you saying you'd even be able to take vacation during the time I'm in Alaska? After being in Mexico part of the summer and fall, you'd be taking off with me in November?"

"No, I probably wouldn't. But when I do have vacation time, you'll already have taken yours."

"You think I'd turn down a trip with you for pleasure if I could possibly manage it? I'll be thrilled to go with you on vacation. So far, I haven't heard any offers from you."

"It's the principle."

"That's what I thought. And you know I want to help Rose by finding out anything I can about her father's murder—I wouldn't call that *pleasure* exactly."

Neither of us has touched our after-dinner liqueur. The argument has turned into a power struggle, no more, no less. Maybe for once we can stick with it long enough to get that out in the open.

"Do you know Paul Lundy called and wanted to know when I was coming up from San Antonio to see you? I told him I was coming late tonight and going back early tomorrow."

"Oh? When did you tell him that—about coming up late tonight?"

"Earlier in the week."

"When you were still telling me you were coming up by six so we could spend more time together?"

"It had nothing to do with you. I didn't want him assuming I could spend my time in Eternal on his business when he could easily come down to interview me."

"And you were still sore about his asking me to give you a message, right?"

"Right. Look, could we turn in now? It's been a pretty long day for me."

I hate this.

chapter 16

....

E-mail from: Ruby
To: Nan
Subject: *The Deep Freeze*

Well, I don't have to go to Alaska to feel iced in—Ed was
out of here early this morning and we made no headway
at all about anything important. I can't believe he's not
being cooperative with the police about Herman's murder
just because he's jealous of Paul—that's just too juvenile.
Not that I imagine he has much to contribute on that
score, since he only had one conversation with Herman
that he didn't even classify as an interview.

Do you think I should encourage Paul to go down and
see him? I certainly don't want anything left unturned because of me—Rose needs some answers.

....

E-mail from: Nan
To: Ruby
Subject: *Temperature Check*

So you had a rotten time? You're writing me about the police matter and ignoring what I wanted to hear more.

No, I don't think Paul's interest in interviewing Ed is your responsibility one way or another. Let them work it out. If I must take sides, I'd say that Ed's right. If Paul wants him, he should go down to see him or order him up to Eternal or whatever he has the power to do. And if Paul's been putting it off, maybe Ed's help isn't that important at this point.

· ·

E-mail from: Ruby
To: Nan
Subject: *Re Temperature Check*

You're right. I'll stay out of it—I'm just annoyed with Ed for lots of other reasons.

Answers. I always have a good time on a certain level simply laying eyes on him, so yeah, we had a good time. But he's being totally unreasonable about my going to Alaska—he came up with some crazy idea that I should have planned a trip to be away at the same time he was or not gone away at all. Then he acted as if I were refusing to vacation with him after Mexico, when I'd like nothing better. He and I both know that he's not going to take a personal trip with me right after a long business journey. He'll have meetings up the wazoo when he gets back, and will be pulling overtime writing up his notes. It's actually an ideal time for me to be away.

· ·

E-mail from: Nan
To: Ruby
Subject: *Calm Down*

Wow—I guess there really is trouble in paradise. These trips to Alaska and Mexico don't dovetail exactly, do they?

And just for the record, you're not thinking of canceling, are you?

••

E-mail from: Ruby
To: Nan
Subject: *No Way, José*

Of course I'm not canceling. We live in separate towns, and at this point, Ed and I don't always see one another even once a month—not exactly a lifetime commitment.

And no, our trips won't dovetail. Assuming he comes back when he said he would, I'd have time to see him before I left for Alaska. Look, if I really thought he'd make lots of room for me when he returned, that would be one thing, but I don't believe that for a minute. We'd more likely spend that same couple of days together after his trip, and then I'd be on my own until his big story got written.

When I told you I wasn't canceling, you agreed with me, didn't you?

••

E-mail from: Nan
To: Ruby
Subject: *Pun Intended*

I think you'd be nuts to stay home. Something tells me this is going to be one *cool* trip.

chapter
17

....

Rose has invited me to be a substitute mom for her at the Bar/Bat Mitzvah parents' meeting tonight, and I'm touched that she felt close enough to ask. Herman's granddaughter, Jackie, is a favorite of mine, and I know her father, Ray, works evenings, so I'm glad to help. Rose is still a basket case, and this parent/child event is something she could afford to miss.

Jackie and I visited the pizza parlor earlier—her first choice of dining establishments—and we're now seated in a semicircle on folding chairs in Temple Rita's Blumberg Social Hall. Kevin's holding forth in informal mode, which to him means a sport coat instead of a suit, and the inevitable black wing tips. Everyone else is in short sleeves. Since he's constantly searching for ways to reach the kids on their own level, I could suggest he take off the tie or wear a sport shirt, but it wouldn't do any good. He says they need to experience *The Rabbi,* so that's what we're all doing.

"Ladies and gentlemen, we're not meeting about arrangements tonight.

"We're taking part in a survey I've prepared, and I'm planning to send the results to other congregations in our area. At the same time, this exercise will bring us closer together. I might even write an article about this for a religious journal."

Wow—he must be really excited to do some writing on his own. This is a first.

"I want to ask you to all push away your chairs and stand in the center of the room. I can see that some of us in this class are late for the meeting, but we're not waiting for procrastinators and laggards."

I'm shocked that he's so bold, and then I see why. Essie Sue's not here with the twins. Maybe they couldn't come up from Buda tonight.

No such luck.

"I heard that, Rabbi, and I'm insulted at your lack of compassion. These two industrious boys have traveled for miles just to be here, and you're calling them *laggards.* And me. I think you should apologize."

"I'm sorry, Essie Sue. I wouldn't have called you that if you'd been here."

"Well, duh . . ."

"Who said that?" Kevin's swirling toward the back of the crowd, but no one confesses.

"Can we please talk about it another time, Essie Sue? You're ruining my big plans."

"Carry on, Rabbi. We'll discuss it later."

She wages an endless war between wanting control and needing to give Kevin the appearance of control, and sometimes it gets out of hand. Like now, when his whining isn't helping the illusion. The kids, of course, have no trouble knowing who's boss.

Kevin had better get us organized fast, because Larry and Lester, who do much better being anchored to chairs, are stirring the waters as our straggly little group stands in the middle of the social hall. They've produced a mini-

Frisbee out of nowhere, and have attracted most of the boys. Jackie and three of her friends are looking down in disgust from the heights of seventh-grade female maturity.

"See what we have to put up with, Ruby?"

I guess she's had a class already with the twins since I last saw her.

"Do something, Kevin," I *noodge* discreetly.

"Gentlemen, gentlemen—put that Frisbee away. Parents, help settle down your children. This is going to be a fun evening."

Oh yeah. The gentlemen-children are temporarily subdued, while the adults in the crowd mill around in a manner I'd consider threatening if I were Kevin.

"Okay, this is the way the game works. I want you all to close your eyes, make a circle, and face inward toward the middle of the circle."

A bad start. I wouldn't trust this crowd with my eyes wide open.

"You, too, Essie Sue."

She gives him one more glare, but obeys, as do I. But then we all discover that with our eyes closed, we can't make a very good circle, much less turn inward.

"You told us backward, Rabbi," Essie Sue says. "Let us make the circle first."

"Whatever. Just do it."

We're evidently geometrically challenged, but we finally coalesce into a semblance of a circle. Only Kevin would be undaunted by this performance.

"This is an identity survey. While you have your eyes closed, I'm walking around and putting four signs in the corners of the room. Now on the count of three, I'm going to call out the words that appear on each of the signs. You're supposed to run to the corner of the room that contains the word most related to your identity."

"I don't get it." This is Larry, followed by Lester, who also doesn't get it.

"You can't understand until I read the words out. Just be patient."

He has as much chance of achieving patience as the zookeepers at meat-throwing time.

Essie Sue raises her hand. "How can we run to the corners of the room until we think about it? You have to give us a few minutes."

"No. The whole point of this exercise is that you have to be spontaneous. If you think too much about it, my survey will be ruined. This is supposed to be your basic identity."

Three more hands go up, but Kevin wisely ignores them.

"Okay, these are the words. On the count of three, you can run. The words are *Jew, American, Human Being,* and *Male/Female.* Now, run."

"With our eyes closed or open?"

"Open."

"You didn't say one, two, three."

He says it and we run.

Five minutes and a few collisions later, we're all congregated more or less in the four corners of the hall. In my corner, mostly less.

Essie Sue's pointing at me from across the room. "Ruby, why are you standing there all by yourself?"

"This is where I'm supposed to be. I'm a female of the species."

Apparently, the only one. There's one more male standing beside me—Hal Margolis, who has temporarily escaped his wife Essie Sue's notice, I guess.

"Hal, bring Ruby over here with the Jews, please."

"What do you mean, bring her over? This is her corner. I'm a male and she's a female."

"Don't be silly. Bring her along on your way over. Rabbi, go see what's the matter with Ruby—Hal can't make her come to the right corner."

Kevin's obviously thrilled that his game is working— he's busy scribbling away in a notebook and visiting the groups gathered under each sign. Except for the twins—they're running around in the middle of the room.

"Hold on, Essie Sue," he says, "I'm busy coordinating everyone. Stay in your places, ladies and gentlemen, and I'll explain the results to you."

I take a quick look around and size up the group. There were twenty-eight of us at the meeting, not counting Kevin. As far as I can see, there are now twelve Jews, eight Americans, four Human Beings, one Male and one Female. And the twins, who I guess defy description.

"Okay, now—I want you all to think about why you feel basically identified with your group."

"You said we weren't supposed to think."

"That was then. This is now—you ran to your corners letting your unconscious tell you where to go. That's what it says in this sociology book. Now we're going to talk about it and see why you went there."

I wonder what sociology book—Kevin's not known for his originality.

"Ruby and Hal, you're the smallest group. Why are you there?"

Hal votes for me to represent our group. Going against Essie Sue is giving him enough to worry about.

"I'm in this corner," I say, "because although I don't go through life saying 'I'm female,' when I compare it to the other three choices, male and female are part of our most basic cellular structure. My origin is female before it's anything else listed here, just as Hal's is male. With that taken for granted, I'm then an American Jew."

"That's crazy. You're a Jew first, before a woman." Essie Sue's waving her hand to be recognized, but of course is already giving her opinion in case she isn't. "Especially you, Ruby. You're a rabbi's wife. You should be ashamed of yourself. You should all be ashamed of yourselves if you're not lined up to be Jews. How are we going to count on you for fund-raising if you're not identifying?"

Before I can assure her that my most basic identity has nothing to do with my giving patterns, Kevin avoids disaster by calling on the Human Beings.

Bubba Copeland is a Human Being—at least he says he is.

"Ruby and Hal are wrong. The basic building block is Human Being—that comes before male or female."

"No, it doesn't," I say. "Separating yourselves from the animal kingdom doesn't sound basic to me. The concept of sexual distinction includes most living beings, not just the human race."

Essie Sue's not letting this go, either. "Human Beings? That sounds Unitarian, and you're Temple members. This is a disgrace."

"And where did we get into this sexual distinction business?" Mrs. Goldberg asks. "If that's like sexual dysfunction, I don't think it should be a part of a religious discussion."

I open my mouth to explain the concept, then close it. Who do I think I'm dealing with? Fortunately, I'm saved by other voices.

"The Americans haven't been heard from, Rabbi."

"Well, neither have the Jews, except that Essie Sue's been speaking out of turn," Kevin says. "Let's have a little order here. Americans first."

"We're one hundred percent American," Mr. Chernoff says. "This is our flag, we served our country, that's it."

The Americans all clap.

"It's our turn now," Essie Sue says. "See how many people lined up here? God made us Jews and that's our basic identity. And last I heard, the majority rules in this country. We win. Where's our prize?"

"There's no winner." Kevin's losing control of the crowd, especially since they've also found out there's no prize. The groups are crossing the lines to make their points, and as a card-carrying female, I'm about to run for safety.

"If the Americans can get your twin cousins on our side, Essie Sue, we'd only be two down," Brother Copeland says. "Then we could persuade two of the Human Beings to come over."

"Nothing doing. Come over here, Larry and Lester. It's time to quit playing and line up with the Jews. We'll take care of your cousin Hal's defection when we get home."

"Hold on," Kevin says. "This isn't a negotiation, it's a survey. Just let them play and don't spoil my strategy for helping the class and parents get to know one another."

"Strategy? You've wasted so much time that I haven't had a chance to firm up my reception plans." She's pulling on the twins, but they won't move.

Larry and Lester shake her off and come up to the front of the room. "We want to be counted in the game," Larry says.

"Then why weren't you in a corner with the Jews?" Essie Sue says.

"Because that's not our basic identification."

"So what are you?" Kevin asks.

"We're Longhorns. We identify with the University of Texas football team."

Each raises a hand with the Hook'em Horns symbol, which looks like the flip side of an obscene gesture—two middle fingers held down by the thumb, with the first and fourth digits waving in the air like—well, like longhorns.

Since everyone else in the room is a Longhorn fan, too, I can see indecision spreading through the crowd like a prairie fire. A few people move toward the middle, with more about to follow.

No one is more aware of this than Kevin, who quickly adjourns the meeting before he has to report twenty-eight Longhorns as the culmination of his survey.

chapter
18

....

"There's no way you're going to Alaska for two weeks, Ruby. You have promises to keep."

While she's lecturing me, Essie Sue is attempting the impossible task of putting fresh creamery butter on her hot poppy seed bagel without anyone seeing her.

"What are you covering up with your napkin, Essie Sue?" Since Milt can't be distracted by mere conversation, he isn't taking his eyes off her.

"I thought you were on your weight-loss kick—campaigning for bare-faced bagels last time you were in here," he says. "By the time I realized you were working the crowd, I'd lost a morning's cream cheese business, special flavors and all."

"I am not spreading butter, Milt Aboud," she says as she crumples up the bagel in her napkin. "What I do with my hands is none of your business."

"I saw you snitching some of the rabbi's cranberry-nut cream cheese a minute ago, too. You quick-dipped your bagel in it."

"I did not. You know my views about what goes on in

this bakery. You and Ruby are fostering an unhealthy lifestyle, and bagels without topping will go a long way toward thinning out the population."

"Ha! It'll be thinned out, all right. Nobody will come here. It'll be unhealthy for our pocketbooks."

"I think she means making people thinner if they don't eat the cream cheese," Kevin says.

"Yeah, like my family starving." Milt pours us more steaming Kenya coffee.

"We know what she means, Kevin," I say.

I'm trying to ward off an outburst, but my delight over Milt's catching Essie Sue in the act doesn't let me quit. "We're just pointing out that her bagels aren't where her mouth is. The cream cheese is."

She pushes everything away, including the coffee. "I know what you're trying to do, Ruby. You think if you can fabricate lies about me, you'll distract me from what I was saying about your trip to Alaska."

"I can open that napkin you pushed aside," Milt says. "Then we'll see who's lying about the butter."

"Just try it," Essie Sue says.

Milt doesn't try it, and it's not because she's cowed him, either. I see him looking at her red lipstick all over the smooshed-up napkin. It presents a formidable barrier to any search.

Dumb he isn't. Nevertheless, Milt's rare opportunity to prove that she's as vulnerable as the rest of us when tempted by our fabulous deli toppings has emboldened me.

"I'm not breaking any promises, Essie Sue. The kids can still stay at my house if you don't want them disturbing Hal's sleep. You'll just have to stay with them for the two weekends I'm gone."

"Unacceptable."

"I thought you said you needed space, not baby-sitting. I'm renting you the space, and I'll even stay with them when I'm not busy, but that's all you're getting out of the deal."

"It is odd, Ruby," Kevin says. "Alaska in the wintertime?"

"There are reasons for that, but I don't owe you two any explanations. Take it or leave it."

"Maybe the rabbi can stay with them," Milt says.

Good. That'll teach Kevin to gang up on me.

"No, I need my rest for services. Count me out."

"Why try to solve everything now?" I say. "Maybe they'll stay in Buda for those weekends."

"Never. They need their Bar Mitzvah training. Maybe your idea of having the rabbi stay with them has merit. He can give them special attention."

The idea of bonding with Lester and Larry doesn't appear to be allaying Kevin's fears. He's just paled three shades, and I can see why.

"I've never had children, Essie Sue. I have no parenting skills."

"Of course you do," she says. "How about all that counseling training that was part of your rabbinic education? Preparation for religious-school teaching."

"We learned what to tell them, not how to take care of them. And I didn't do so great on the first part of that."

This we know all too well.

"I think I can be a better spiritual guide if I don't live with them," he says finally. "And besides, they're bigger than I am."

I'm caught between wanting to remind Essie Sue of Kevin's last excursion at the mall with the boys and my own self-interest in getting out of town. Self-interest is about to win when she changes her mind without prodding. Maybe my ESP got through to her.

"I can't deal with this right now—I'm putting it on hold for tomorrow."

Thank you, Scarlett.

Meanwhile, Milt's about to backtrack—I can tell. He's probably afraid of our losing the rent money at a time when the bakery's cash poor.

"Look on the good side, Essie Sue. Ruby's going to salmon country. She might be able to track down a bargain for you up there."

I plotz. She doesn't need to know my plans to investigate. "Not a good idea, Milt. We're covering Kodiak Island as well as the Denali area and Fairbanks. I'll have no time for fish shopping."

Too late. Her eyes are gleaming already.

"Okay, Ruby, it's a deal. If you can get me some discounted smoked salmon, you can go and I'll still pay the rent."

I momentarily put my hands over my ears and glare at Milt, who looks unchastened.

"You and Ruby can nail this down later," he says.

All thought of the twins' welfare seems to have flown out the window now that there's a bargain in sight.

"You can take Herman's place, Ruby, and make my food arrangements for me. Maybe they have other things we can use, too. How about herring?"

"What do you think Alaska is," I say, "a refrigerated deli case?"

Unfortunately, she's lost to me. The only answer I get is her mantra: "Wholesale. At the source."

chapter
19

....

I can't believe Kevin's the one driving me to the air-port, but he called to offer last night and I accepted. I appreciate it, but I'm hoping there are no strings attached—he seldom goes out of his way for me without a reason. In fact, he's whining already and I just got in the car. Surely he didn't volunteer to take me just so he'd have a last chance to gripe.

"It's not fair, Ruby, that I have to live over at your house on the weekends, but Essie Sue's making me. She says Hal's care is more important than my comfort, can you believe it? She makes it sound as if the guy's an invalid."

I suspect she simply doesn't want to be away from home when Kevin can do the dirty work for her, and it'll mean she can take a break from the imperious twins. I'm not saying too much, though—my main purpose is to get out of town, not to have Kevin quoting me to Essie Sue.

"It's only two weekends, and you only have to sleep there at night. You can hold it together for that long, can't you? What can happen?"

He looks at me. Even *I* can't make that remark with a straight face, but I'm hiding it.

"Just do me one favor, Kevin—please don't leave them alone in my house, okay?"

Oy Vay is staying with Milt and Grace while I'm gone—I'm not abandoning any living being to who knows what. I'm not worried about Oy Vay's holding her own with the boys—not at her size—but I don't want her to have the aggravation.

"It'll be their bedtime by the time I come over," he says—"all I've agreed to do is stay overnight."

"Can we change the subject?" I'm beginning to be sorry I didn't take a cab.

"You certainly don't look like you're headed for the frozen North, Ruby."

"I'm borrowing fur-lined boots and a Gore-Tex parka from Nan's friend when I get to Seattle. She's bringing them to the airport for me."

"You're not staying there? I thought that's where you were doing the food shopping for Essie Sue."

"I hate to break it to you, Kevin, but this trip isn't planned around Essie Sue—it's my vacation. I adore Seattle, but we didn't have time for a real visit tacked on to the Alaska trip, so we're taking off as soon as I get there. I packed every sweater I own, and some long underwear from Bean. Lots of wool socks, too—my backpack's overstuffed."

I can see he's not interested, so I might as well figure out the purpose of this favor.

"Thanks for taking me to the airport—I appreciate it."

"You're welcome."

"How come you decided to ask me?"

I realize this question would be an affront to most of us, but not to Kevin. He's not smooth enough to pretend he's shocked that I'd question his motives—especially when he *has* motives.

"I had to go to the police station yesterday to review a statement I made that was confusing. I straightened it out in about a minute. Then Lieutenant Lundy asked me in passing if you'd broken up with your boyfriend—he said he thought you might have. I wanted to be the first one to tell Essie Sue, since she's always saying I'm not up on any-thing. But if I'm wrong, it'd be worse than not telling her at all. I hated to wait two weeks until you come back—it might be old by then."

Well, at least he's straightforward, but I get a big ping in the middle of my chest anyway. This is not what I need as my send-off.

"Paul Lundy? What's he got to do with this?"

"He asked Ed Levinger to keep him posted on his travel schedule in case he needed to ask him any more questions about the article Herman Guenther wanted him to write. Ed told Paul he was coming back from Mexico while you were still in Alaska, and he didn't seem happy about it. Paul had assumed Ed would be up here in Eternal seeing you as soon as he got back from Mexico."

"So from this Paul assumed we'd broken up? What busi-ness is it of his, and why did he bring something like that up with you?"

I really don't get it. Now all of a sudden Ed and Paul are buddy-buddy, when they'd been circling each other for months?

"He was asking me because he thought I might know."

"Which means he didn't know himself, right?"

"Yeah, he was pumping me for information. As if you ever tell me anything. I thought if I took you to the airport you might let me be the one to know the lowdown. As your spiritual leader."

"Oh yes, you'd be just the one I'd use to spread the word, Kevin. This might come as a surprise to you, but people usually *confide* in their spiritual leader. That means he doesn't let everyone know."

"I won't tell."

"There's nothing *to* tell. Maybe you should ask Ed—he seems to be the one talking about it."

"Never mind. That'll be too late—Essie Sue will probably know by then one way or the other."

"Well, gee, I hope she gives me the news, too. I don't know who to be more annoyed with, Ed or Paul."

Uh-oh—I seem to be thinking aloud here—it's easy to do that with Kevin, but he took me by surprise. I need to keep my mouth shut around him.

"I think Paul likes you, too, Ruby."

"Well, he has a great way of showing it, don't you think?"

"Are you mad at him?"

"Why?"

Thankfully, we're pulling up at the curb of the departure area at the Austin airport.

"Well, if you don't like either one of them, you could always get back together with me."

"But we were never together, Kevin."

"We dated once. I almost kissed you in this very car."

"*Oy*. That was an arranged date years ago, and you need to concentrate on the *almost* part."

That's the nicest thing I can think to say about that truly appalling night. I thank him, jump out of the car almost as fast as I did then, and grab my enormous backpack from the backseat.

Wow—do I need a vacation.

chapter
20

....

Nan's waiting for me on the spacious indoor bridge leading from the stacked parking lots to the main building of the Seattle/Tacoma airport. In the course of a few hours I've made two plane connections on my journey west and finished up by squeezing into one of the underground railcars zipping back and forth between terminals. The Japanese travelers so visible here don't usually carry backpacks, and understandably consider it an affront to move aside in order to avoid being knocked down by mine.

None of which bothers us as we hug like two unwieldy hunchbacks. She immediately unloads a huge red parka on me, and a pair of winter boots.

"I brought them in the car separate," she says. "Now you can lug them."

"Thanks," I tell her. "You look great. I can't believe it's been this long since we've seen each other."

Lawyering apparently agrees with her. She's lost that vaguely chaotic look she wore throughout her law student years, when everything she did seemed to be preceded and followed by long lists of things she needed to do and hadn't done.

"You're looking pretty good, yourself. I think you're finally making it back into the land of the living, Ruby. Stu would be proud of you."

Hearing this means a lot to me, but I didn't mean to show it by bursting into tears.

"Yeah, I think I'm through it. The only way I can tell is that at last I'm able to look back and see it whole—whatever *it* is."

"Let's really celebrate. I don't think this trip is going to be too difficult professionally, and I intend to take as much time off as I can get away with—which should be a lot. We have two weeks to gab and catch up."

"We're talking as though we haven't kept the phone wires and the modems burning several times a week," I say.

"It's different in person. I'm just glad to lay my eyes on you, babe."

Alaska Airlines tells us we have to check the behemoths on our backs, even though I insist I was allowed to carry mine onboard the other airline. I'm ready to ask for the supervisor when Nan pats me on the shoulder.

"Give it up, Ruby. You're on vacation, remember? You don't have to make everything a negotiation."

She's right, of course. Nan can not only see right through me most of the time but also has the uncanny ability to let me look, too. Not that I always like what I see. This time, I shut up and hand over my bag after first stuffing it with the winter boots and the parka.

"Are you two sisters?" the ticket person asks. We're used to this.

"Only soul sisters," Nan says.

"Well, you sure look alike."

Nan has the same firm build as I do, and her hair is auburn, too. Plus, we're the same height—five foot five.

She's letting her hair grow out right now while my curls are cut short as usual, but I guess the resemblance is still there. And our taste in clothes is the same—very convenient on trips when we might have forgotten something.

We have an aisle seat and a window. Our usual modus operandi is to hope for the best, and then switch seats if a third person shows up—they're always more than happy to have one of us sit in the middle. So far our luck is holding, and we stash our books and extras in the seat between us for now. It's hot onboard, and we strip off our sweaters.

"I could hardly bring myself to dress for the freezing weather today," Nan says. "We're having our usual Pacific Northwest November—rain and a chill in the air, but nothing approaching real winter."

"Ha—how would you like to start out from Texas in the low eighties—we're having an unusual hot spell. Of course, in my opinion, what's unusual is when we *don't* have an unusual hot spell. We don't have mountains, though. I'd give anything to see Mount Rainier again," I say as we take off.

"No chance," she says, "unless we have to circle back a bit and part of it is sticking through the thick clouds."

As if on cue, I see the smooth, snowy top of Rainier out a tiny corner of my window, looking exactly like one of the clouds surrounding it. I consider it a lucky omen.

Nan's staying in Anchorage for her first hearings, and I'm going to Kodiak Island alone. She'll fly down to meet me for a day or so when she's finished, so she can at least lay her eyes on Kodiak. I'm sorry to have to incur the extra hotel expenses on my own there, but since I'm tagging along to check out the fish distributors as well as to vacation, it's the best plan I can come up with.

We're late landing in Anchorage, so all we see is our airport arrival lounge and an attendant waving me toward a small terminal. I'm suddenly very happy to have checked my backpack in Seattle. I have what seems like no time to say good-bye to Nan and run for the plane.

The small size of the jet to Kodiak Island surprises me, though I don't know why it should—I ought to be thankful it's not a prop plane. I have a seat near the pilot, who looks like he's twenty. I tell myself he's got to be older than that to have this job. At least, I hope so.

The flight attendant examines my seat belt herself—that's a first. "Ever flown into Kodiak?" she asks. When I say no, she smiles to herself and moves down the aisle. I don't like the look of that smile. I try to concentrate on that earlier sighting of Mount Rainier that I considered a lucky omen—I might need it. I look out the window and realize it's late afternoon, which, in early November, means it's practically dark outside.

The flight south of Anchorage is short and choppy, but tolerable. During World War II, Kodiak Island served as a supply center for the Aleutian Islands, southwest of the mainland. I'm amazed at how close it is to the Bering Sea, but of course I can't see much beyond the clouds. It's not until we're low enough to see the lights on the island that things get hairy.

"Hold on, folks," the pilot says. "We're on our way in."

I'm wondering where's he supposed to land. The runway lights look as though they're right at the water's edge.

The jet seems to cut power abruptly. It drops almost down to the water and then rises up again so fast that I'm glued to the back of my seat.

"Didn't make it that time. Maybe next go-round," the pilot says over the loudspeaker.

We passengers can only stare at one another. After three more attempts, each steeper and scarier than the last, we finally touch down on the island.

The flight attendant emerges from her own seat near the door and tells us we've arrived.

"Was that some kind of emergency landing?" I ask.

"Emergency? No. Landing in Kodiak is always tight. Barometer Mountain's right there at the end of the runway."

I see nothing, but who cares? All I want to do is get off the plane.

The temperature's in the thirties when I climb down, and although there's some old snow on the ground, it's clear outside. I realize it was foolhardy to pack my parka, but I'm close to the terminal.

My heart's still spasming as I take off in a cab for the city of Kodiak, five miles around Pillar Mountain. I'm not too nervous to notice the spruce and cottonwood trees I've researched, and I can actually see a couple of bald eagles perched on the branches.

The cabbie fills me in on the infamous Kodiak grizzly bears, the largest in the world. He seems to relish telling me that they occasionally venture from the backcountry to town, and that they're even larger than the stuffed bear in the glass case at the airport. But after that daredevil descent earlier, I'm unfazed. I figure if I survived that, I can take anything the rest of Alaska can hand out. As usual, I don't know what I'm talking about.

chapter
21
....

I've had a ball exploring the island while Nan's been in her meetings in Anchorage, though I'm sorry she's missed so much. There's nothing to do at night, but I've been so tired that it hasn't mattered. I usually have an early supper and turn in. What's most surprising to me is that it's sometimes difficult to get a good fish dinner, and yet Kodiak is the base of a multimillion-dollar fishing fleet. The processing plants on the harbor front are devoted to the big-time movement of fish in refrigerated cargo vans, not to supplying the local eateries, so most of the fish is exported. Although, if I had rented an apartment, I could have bought fresh fish in season at the supermarket.

I'm also on my own in another way, since the tourist business thrives in the warmer seasons, not now. One day I did find a man who's a tour guide in the summer, and he drove me to some of the more inaccessible villages. The roads define the populated portion of the island—the rest is wilderness. Two thirds of the place is a national wildlife refuge, and November, in my opinion, is no time to think of hiking, even if I had the time.

Today I'm hanging out at the waterfront, not far from my hotel. This trip has been just what I needed—I can truly say I haven't thought of home more than a few minutes a day since I arrived. Too much to do and see.

Unfortunately, I looked at the calendar this morning and realized this is the day Ed returns from Mexico. I'm so far north I can't even picture what it must be like in Eternal today, much less Mexico. Warm, I'm sure, even in November. I love the cold weather here, possibly because I know my time will come to an end soon. I suppose he's still annoyed that I'm not home to see him, though I wonder how soon he'd actually find time to get up to Eternal if I *were* home. Our last meeting in late September was disappointing—we were both cranky-trying-to-be-nice, and that never works. But I missed him like crazy when he left. I don't know what I would have done if I hadn't had Alaska to look forward to.

I'm also well aware that my big plan was to check on fish distributors here in Kodiak, despite the fact that I'm glorying in forgetfulness. I have the address of the Acme Jobbers of Seattle and Kodiak, and my goal today is to find the place.

Fishing boats line the loading docks—there's a brisk breeze, but my wool hat is snug over my ears and I'm not even cold enough to pull up the hood of my parka. There's no letdown of activity here during the fall/winter season. I'm fascinated with the procession of boats unloading cargo from the fish holds. Giant cranes and then forklifts carry the fish totes into the processing plants to be prepared for cooking or freezing.

Summer is salmon season, so I doubt if I can easily locate Acme Jobbers unless they also process winter products. The address of the fishery indicates that it's not too far, so I zip up my parka and keep walking along the harbor. A small entranceway sticks out from what I think is the building I'm looking for, and I open the door and go in.

A young woman's on the phone—she gives me a slight smile and points toward the coffeemaker and a stack of Styrofoam cups. I pour myself half a cup of coffee so black and thick I could stand the spoon in it, but hey, it's hot, and I'm not complaining. She's on the phone for a long time, but I have no schedule to meet.

"Is this Acme Jobbers?" I ask when she's finished.

"It shares part of the plant. They're salmon."

"And that's summer, right?" I want her to know that at least I'm *that* well informed, though not much beyond. Instead, I might as well have put a dunce cap on myself.

She gives me the nonverbal equivalent of "Duh" and asks me what I want. Since I'm not sure, I finesse by pointing to a poster on the wall. It shows sockeye salmon in a stream, which wouldn't be unusual except for the fact that these salmon are literally wall-to-wall across the riverbed—you could walk over them like a land bridge.

"That's amazing," I say. "Are they really that thick here in the summer season?" Now that I've shown my ignorance, I figure I'll capitalize on it by being a total tourist and throwing myself on her mercy.

"Yep. In July and August, the salmon swim in the rivers and jump in the bays. People here just lean down and grab 'em. After four or five years, the fish swim back to the same stream where they were born."

I open my mouth to respond, but she interrupts.

"There's books about it in the gift shop two streets back." She's pointing my way out of here, obviously deciding she's done her tourist bit for the morning.

"I'll get one, but I came in here because I'm a customer of yours in Texas."

"You'll have to talk to Moe. He's in back."

"Back here?" I'm on my way before she can pick up the phone.

There's only one office in back, at the head of a long corridor leading, I imagine, to the plant floor. I barge in and ask the man inside if he's Moe. He looks like a football tackle.

"Yeah. How'd you get in here?"

"The person in front said you were back here," I say. I'm relieved she didn't find it necessary to chase after me.

"We don't allow visitors in the plant. Some of the other places have tours, but not us. We're not even operating now." He lights a big, black cigar and blows the smoke in my face for emphasis.

"I'm from Texas, and I'm co-owner of a place near Austin called The Hot Bagel. My partner is Milt Aboud, and we were getting our salmon from Acme Jobbers. We were having some problems."

"Wait, lady. This is the source. What you want is the distributor."

"But your letterhead lists Seattle and Kodiak. There was a man named Herman Guenther who worked with us and who had some correspondence with you I wanted to check out. I . . ."

The phone rings and he reaches for it.

Like the woman in front, he points to his coffeepot, so I assume I'm in for a long wait. I'm not ready to swill that coffee, though, so I take out a notepad and look busy.

I'm almost spaced out after listening to a one-sided conversation about late orders and cleaning supplies, when I suddenly perk up.

"There's a lady here from Texas who says she's a customer and has some problem with us."

I quickly scribble some more information on my notepad and hand it to him.

"She tells me we deal with a man named Milt Aboud and one called Herman Guenther. And she says that Mr. Guenther's recent murder is the subject of a police investigation, and they've been going through his papers."

Something's going on at the other end, but I can't tell what.

"I have no idea why she's down here in Kodiak." He chomps on the cigar and looks past me as if I weren't there.

"He says who are you?"

I tell him I'm Ruby Rothman of The Hot Bagel, and he duly reports it.

He talks for a few more minutes about other business and hangs up.

"That's my boss. They say you should talk to Seattle about problems. He knows nothing about a Mr. Guenther."

"But that was only one of the things I wanted to talk about. I wanted to know if you could fill a special order at the beginning of next salmon season."

"Orders and problems are Seattle. Kodiak's not busy this time of year."

"Can I have your name and the name of the person you talked to about me?"

"My name's Moe Sands. If you write, just tell them you talked to me and what I said about orders and problems."

"Could you show me around?" I figure I might as well try.

"No."

Moe stands up and pretty much moves me out the door by looming so close to me that I have to go forward to get out of his way. We continue this physical good-bye until I'm up the corridor, into the waiting room, and out the front door.

chapter

22

∙∙∙∙∙∙∙∙∙∙∙∙∙∙∙∙∙∙∙∙∙∙

"Surely you're not lining up these fish people to keep supplying The Hot Bagel? I wouldn't want to touch their products after what happened with Herman."

Nan's hearing in Anchorage ended this morning and she took the short flight down to join me. We're enjoying great halibut at a restaurant on the waterfront. Since I know halibut is harvested in the spring and summer, I'm pretty sure this must be frozen, but it's fluffy and delicious and utterly unlike any I've ever had. The waitress asked if we'd like reindeer steak, but out of respect for Judeo-Christian relations, we declined to eat anything that might ever have brought holiday presents to little children. She also informed us that Kodiak celebrates two Christmases, the other being the Russian Orthodox celebration.

I take a bite of a pretty good hot roll and answer Nan's question about the fish people.

"Of course I'm not planning to buy salmon from Acme Jobbers. Milt's already made plans to switch to another supplier—I just wanted an *in* with them here so I could possibly get some information about Herman. I'm sure they don't get threats like his every day."

"But you didn't get anything from them this morning, did you?"

"Not a thing, but you never know when someone will open up to you. If I'd had more time with the woman in the front office, who knows what she might have spilled over lunch?"

"Only her coffee, maybe, and not that if she had half a brain. My guess is these people know nothing—I can't imagine Kodiak being anyone's business hub."

"You're probably right, but this was one of the reasons I came to Alaska, and specifically why I'm in Kodiak. I certainly wasn't going to be all the way up here and not check out the local address I had. Now it's done."

"If you remember, Ruby, my private detective friend didn't come up with anything, either, when he asked around for you in Seattle."

"No, but at that point I didn't want him involving the bakery—he just asked anonymous questions about Herman. Today I had to put us into the mix if I wanted an excuse to drop in there."

We ask for more tea and are told it's a special Russian recipe from the restaurant's owner. Kodiak was the first Russian settlement in Alaska, and the leading families and main streets still bear Russian names. The Russian stories go all the way back to the late seventeen hundreds, and every merchant we've run into has told us we should be here in August, when a famous historical pageant brings in hordes of tourists.

Only one museum attendant I ran into went beyond the Russians to emphasize the indigenous heritage of Kodiak. The native Koniag peoples survived slaughter by the Russians and the usual conversions and conquests to leave their own legacy on the island, and I bought a beautiful soapstone carving by one of them—a native artist. I wish

Nan had been able to see more sights with me, but she had her own problems.

"The hearings were a lot more complicated than we bargained for, Ruby. I had to do research on the fly to counteract what the other side came up with."

"I'd be glad to help for the upcoming Fairbanks hearing if you'd just tell me details. You know I'm good at this."

"Yeah, I know you'd gladly skip law school and plunge right in, babe, but I told you I can't discuss the facts in the case."

"Your loss—I'm just sorry that you've missed most of Kodiak."

It's killing me that I actually got to see puffins and she didn't, and that I trooped around an area filled with white ash that's lingered ever since Kodiak was engulfed by a volcanic eruption in 1912. My guide told me that their entire waterfront was wiped out by a tidal wave in the 1964 earthquake that devastated central Alaska, and that people on the island now measure time by what happened before and after the disaster.

Our waitress assures us it's all worth it, that she wouldn't live anywhere else. Her ambition, though, is to travel through Mexico, of all places.

"My boyfriend's family is from there," she says. "His father originally came up to work on the pipeline and stayed. But he wants to go back, and he's taking me with him."

"My boyfriend just got back from there," I say.

"Your what?" Nan gives me a look. "I thought you just gave me a disclaimer on that when I was cheeky enough to assume the obvious."

"Maybe he'll call tonight, now that he's back. I left the number of our hotel."

"Why don't you call him?"

"Let him call me first."

"That's mature."

We walk back to the hotel in a thick fog that makes me

shiver, and not just from the cold. It's surreal to picture this big rock of an island swept by winds and pounded by waves, barely surviving the most extreme of natural disasters. And yet, there's a thriving life and history here, and at least one waitress who wouldn't live anywhere else in the world.

When we get back to the hotel, I find a message from Ed.

"See? Told you," Nan says.

"You did? Not that I remember. You told me to call *him*."

"Well, now you won't have to." Amazing how she gets out of everything so easily.

"I'm going in to take a bath. Have a ball without me."

"Thanks. I *am* glad he called first, though."

I settle myself on the bed to phone Ed and emerge into reality twenty minutes later, at the very same moment Nan comes out of the bathroom.

"Amazing coincidence how you timed that," I say. "Thanks again—really."

"Don't mention it. My body's shrunken like a prune, but I'll recover. I used up all the hot water, though, rewarming the tub about fifty times. Now that I've given you your privacy, tell me everything, and don't leave one thing out."

chapter
23

....

I take a quick, lukewarm bath, and we both plop on our beds to yak. Or at least she wants me to yak. I'd rather slide under the covers.

"It's certainly not apparent that the two of you had a fight," Nan says.

"We didn't."

"In fact, you look as if you've just been kissed."

I don't answer.

"Okay, I can see you're gonna be coy with me."

"I'm not being coy—I'm trying to recover."

"Well, tell me *something* already. Is Ed still annoyed with you for coming here?"

"He said he missed me, but other than that, he didn't give me a hard time."

I use the few minutes while Nan's pouting at my reticence to take stock. I know my attitude is a direct result of living alone. I'm so used to being able to process my thoughts in private that it's hard to come to terms with the fact that there's someone else in the room, even if she is my best friend. I try to remember all the times I've wished she *were* around. Plus, I do enough griping with her that I ought to be able to share something less negative for a change.

"He was really very sweet," I say. "He got home last night, and he's laid up with some sort of virus now."

"The usual tourista stomach thing?"

"He doesn't think so, because the food usually doesn't bother him—he's spent lots of time in Mexico. I'm hoping it's nothing serious, like something he might have picked up in the countryside."

"Look, the water can disable the best of them—and especially when they think they're invulnerable."

"He doesn't consider himself invulnerable."

"I'm sorry—I guess I'm being a pill. You don't have to tell me about the conversation as if we were high school girls." Nan reaches over between the beds to swing my hand.

That's all I need to totally dissolve.

"This guy really gets to you, doesn't he, hon?"

"Yeah, and I think he's feeling as chaotic about us as I do."

The truth is I'm really glad to be away, and I've thoroughly enjoyed myself on this trip, so I can imagine how Ed felt about going to Mexico. But he's now the subtext to the vacation, and no matter how hard I might try, he's always going to be there. This brief connection by phone has made it harder, somehow, to pretend he isn't.

I decide I can deal with this more easily if I give Nan facts instead of emotions.

"The business part of his trip went well, and he thinks it's going to make a good investigative piece. He'll start working on it as soon as he can shake this whatever-it-is."

"So do you think if you had stayed home, you'd have been able to see him for a week or so in Eternal?"

"No. He'd be plunging in before the story got cold."

"The relationship sounds less chaotic than sporadic. Any chance the infrequency's what provides the intensity?"

This is the Nan I know and dread.

"I mean well, Ruby—I really do. Don't look at me that way."

"I'm only looking with wonder. Always on target."

"Whether you like it or not, huh?"

"It's hard to get mad at your compass, Nan. Not everybody has someone who tells it straight no matter what."

"I only wish I could be as direct with my own life as I am with yours. I guess I depend on you for that."

"Now that we've done the mutual admiration bit, do you think we could talk about the rest of the trip? I really do need some time to think about the conversation with Ed."

"Which, for the record, you still managed to keep mostly to yourself."

She tips her Diet Coke can at me, and we both relax a little while I get out my Alaska maps. I'm a map freak, and have just added an Alaska railroad map to my new collection.

"Wanna hear about the railroad before we think about having to fly out of here?" I ask. "I'm still thinking about that horrible plane trip to the island."

Nan points out that her flight to join me in Kodiak wasn't as scary as my trip had been, and that the return to Anchorage tomorrow should be fine.

Since Nan doesn't have time, I've been appointed travel director for the nonbusiness parts of the journey. Which of course I love. We'll be in Anchorage for a day and a night before going on the train trip north. We're staying for a night at the site of an abandoned gold mine, and then continuing north for Nan's Fairbanks hearing.

I grab my railroad map, spread it on the bed, and point out our final destination, Fairbanks, one hundred twenty miles from the Arctic Circle. The railroad is closer to Russia than to the States, which alone is fascinating to me. Not surprisingly, gold built the railroad, or at least the lure of it did, when the Alaska Central Railroad Company was founded in 1902 as a way for Americans to reach the gold fields of Alaska.

In wintertime, the train is a lifeline to people living between Anchorage and Fairbanks. Summertime is a whole different experience—hordes of tourists board long observation trains to travel through Denali National Park, which contains some of the most beautiful mountain scenery in the world. It's rugged, but the accommodations are sophisticated and civilized.

Since it's winter, we'll be traveling without many tourists. In November, I'm sure there'll be fewer cars chugging up the tracks to the frozen north. The train runs only once a week on this route, and we've planned our trip around its schedule. It operates like the old-fashioned streetcars and picks up travelers on any part of its route. From what I hear, the passengers will be carrying anything from chain saws to fishing rods, supporting their life in the bush. I can't wait.

chapter

24

....

Nan has a big grin on her face as we ease the oversized packs off our backs and wait for our train to arrive at the Anchorage railroad terminal. We're right on time, which is surprising considering how sleep-deprived we are.

I was sorry I had only one day to look around Anchorage after our flight from Kodiak. I'd thought we might take in some nightlife, but I was obviously overreaching. Nan and I took one look at each other at the hotel last night and knew we were going down for the count. But instead of a dreamless sleep until our wake-up call, we tossed the whole night. By the time we left the hotel at eight for the train station, again in total darkness, we looked like something the grizzlies dragged in.

"When's the train coming? We could have slept later," Nan says.

"As if we were sleeping," I say.

"No, I was sleeping, Ruby. It's only that my deepest sleep came right before we got the wake-up call."

There are only two or three scattered prospective passengers waiting with us on the platform, and I decide to drag my backpack over to the iron bench. The only thing coming down the track is a single car, which I guess is doing some sort of maintenance work.

The next thing I see is Nan yanking the big straps across her shoulders and moving toward the little car.

"Come on, Ruby. This is it."

"Hold up," I say. "What is this, anyway? The Little Engine That Could?" I could never have imagined that this sole railway car would operate on subway time, but sure enough, I barely have time to throw my stuff up the train steps before it takes off again.

Naturally, we have no trouble getting adjusted—there's only the one car. We take a front seat, facing the right way, so that we're very close to the closed door of the engine section. The other passengers are near the back, and are already prepared to wrap themselves in blankets to finish out the night.

The conductor looks as though he came from Central Casting—balding, little gray mustache, gold-rimmed glasses, and a potbelly. He tells us the ride might turn out to be a bit more informal than we're used to.

Our railcar is called an RDC, for Rail Diesel Car, and it actually is a little engine that could. It's known all over Alaska as the RDC, and is completely self-contained. It's also the lifeblood of those Alaskans cut off from the rest of the state in winter. People trek from homesteads in what's still called the bush to renew supplies and sometimes change locations. The conductor even hosted a wedding once.

I'm snapping pictures like crazy out the window when he reminds me not to use up all my film—there's much more beautiful scenery ahead. I accept the advice without mentioning that I don't have to worry about film—the camera is digital.

I'm not sure if the train picked up food in Anchorage or whether there's a stove onboard, but we're served great muffins, orange juice, and hot coffee. The other passengers aren't waking up for the treat—maybe they've brought their own food to economize.

Soon we're headed for wilderness. The dots of houses are farther apart until they disappear altogether before we reach the giant Chugach Mountains. Since we're still traveling at sea level, the seven-thousand-foot mountains soar vertically from our vantage point at their base.

"You think this is amazing." Nan looks up from her travel guide. "Just wait until we approach Denali Park."

"It didn't take long for you to get into the tourist spirit, did it?"

"I feel like a free woman—or at least until the Fairbanks hearing," she says.

"And don't forget our stay at the abandoned gold mine before we even reach Fairbanks—that's a vacation in itself."

"I'm amazed you talked the manager into letting us stay there, Ruby—isn't he supposed to be closed this month?"

"Yeah, but I guess he didn't mind making a few bucks as long as he's on the property anyway. He says the Japanese start coming up in December, to see the aurora borealis. If we're lucky, we'll see the sky show, too, even though the northern lights aren't quite as spectacular as they'll be later on."

"I hope he keeps the cabins warm."

As for myself, I'm running out of superlatives just watching the scenery at hand.

The conductor seems thrilled to play tour guide—I guess most of his passengers are locals. He tells us that the worst danger of train travel in winter is moose on the tracks. When snowplows clear the tracks, they create a space where moose can reach the vegetation they're seeking for food. As a result, the moose will suddenly run in front of a train with no warning, and it's too late to stop. I'm praying we don't have any encounters.

Just as Nan and I are beginning to stretch our legs and roam around the car, we're jerked back into the nearest seat when the train stops, seemingly in the middle of nowhere. A true Paul Bunyan type comes aboard carrying a fishing pole, a huge shovel, and three coolers. He's followed by a woman with a tripod and cameras slung around her neck.

We start and stop two more times before we get to Denali, and I don't see any of these passengers paying or showing tickets. A couple of them ride only for one stop.

"I'd love to know where they're going," Nan says. "This is like a city bus."

I can't resist speaking to the photographer. She's from a magazine in Anchorage, doing a story on a gold camp. Many of the old mining sites are now hotels for tourists in the summertime, she says, and she wants to get some winter shots for her story. She tells me the places are totally deserted at this time of year. We've passed Talkeetna, one of the scheduled stops, and the photographer points out that beyond this juncture on our journey almost due north, the railroad is the only way travelers can leave this part of the wilderness. I see rifles and knives all over the place—this is black bear country, and I guess the settlers are prepared.

We're climbing steadily, and I only hope the engine can take it. Suddenly Mount Denali rises before us—the tallest mountain in North America. The climb tapers down at Hurricane Gulch, but soon rises again at Summit.

"We'll never be able to describe this scenery back home," I say. Traveling in winter, with the tracks literally laid out on the permafrost, is beyond words. I walk up to the front cabin to ask the engineer if I can stand beside his chair, and he's glad to have me. He tells me his ancestors are the same Eskimos who once drove dogs over this territory. His hand is poised on the air horn most of the time to warn away the moose.

I notice that one of the men in the back gets up when I go to stand by the engineer. He's not following me—he just seems to check out my location whenever I move.

Since everyone's so friendly, I give him a nod, but he doesn't acknowledge it. I ask the engineer if he knows him, but he doesn't—he says many of the men are sportsmen who come and go.

We see the long summer observation cars parked near the Denali Park station, and I realize from their size that the summer trip here would be an entirely different experience.

My engineer friend warns me to go back to my seat when we leave the park area and continue in the vicinity of the Nenana River.

Nan's relieved to see me.

"They tell me it's hairy at this part of the track," she says, "and that we should stay in our seats."

"You don't know the half of it," I say. "The ride is so precarious here that the train only goes at twenty miles per hour." It's scary just looking out the window when we pass the "million-dollar curve"—called that because it takes millions to support the railroad at this juncture. The mountains are actually moving here, and the tracks with them, so the roadbed must be constantly restructured and supported. So we're rolling on permafrost on a roadbed that's perennially unstable, above one of the most treacherous rivers, the Nenana, in the whole continent. I'm glad I'm in my seat.

When the worst of the hairpin turns have been passed, Nan and I doze off, and don't wake up until it's completely dark again and we're on our way to Fairbanks. We're looking forward to our planned stopover—several stops and many miles before the train's final Fairbanks destination. A driver's supposed to meet us at a prearranged stop. I've done my preliminary checking with the conductor, who's used to worried passengers, and who tells me he'll be sure to stop there. Most of the passengers have long since departed and there are only a few people bound all the way for Fairbanks—probably government or university people this time of year.

As the conductor helps us off the train and says good-bye, I know I'm making a foolish request, but I do it anyway. I ask him to hold up for five minutes while we see if someone's come to pick us up. He says he can't do that, but assures us that the resort is responsible and that there's a working phone at the stop—it's not a full-fledged station, but it's enclosed. I'd even be glad to see the guy in our car who seemed to be checking me out, but unfortunately he's not following us off the train.

So here we are, looking at each other. It's pitch-dark, and we've been told the temperature is about twenty degrees. Two months later and we'd be standing here in sub-zero weather—way subzero—sometimes it's minus fifty here. The snow is deep, though, from a previous snowfall that hasn't melted.

"This was your idea, Ruby. I hope you know what you're doing," Nan says as we find ourselves totally alone in the dark. I can't even see a road. Before I got off the train I secured the hood to my parka and put on my gloves, but now I have to take them off to look in my backpack. Fortunately, I carried a flashlight for reading in bed after Nan had fallen asleep at night.

"Well, it's not windy." That's all I can think of to say. Nan just looks at me, tightening her scarf.

I start looking for a phone in the shelter—we're standing under something that looks like a covered bus stop at home, but it's closed in like a little tin box.

"Yikes—money. Do you have any change?" Nan's pointing her mittens at my waist pack. "Who's going to be the one to take off her mittens and put the coins in?"

"I have coins, but at the moment I'm more interested in where they're going—I don't see any phone."

chapter
25

....

"I'm sure there's a light switch in here, too, but I can't see it or feel it on the wall," I say.

"That's because you have your gloves on."

"Okay, I'll take one off—partway—and hold my flashlight with the other hand." I use my teeth to pull the glove off two fingers, and I run them along the freezing wall while I'm shining my light for the phone.

"I have to go to the bathroom." Nan's doing a little two-step—whether from cold or kidneys, I can't tell. Maybe both.

"Hold it in. I can't even imagine how you'd manage getting out of your snow clothes."

"The odd thing is, Ruby, that when I saw that the train schedule said we'd be here at four o'clock, I absorbed it in Sunbelt time, not this."

"Me, too—actually, I didn't even think about it."

All of a sudden Nan darts outside the shed.

"Lights—I see headlights."

I step outside and see a sweep of light illuminating the

snowy forest across the road from us. The only trouble is that the light's coming from a vehicle headed the other way.

"It took off from a parked position when I went out to look at it," Nan says.

"That's impossible. I didn't see anything parked."

"How could you have seen anything parked if its head-lights weren't on?"

"Well, surely they would have honked at us to let us know they were there."

"Ruby, the cold's getting to your brain cells. This obvi-ously isn't the car or van or whatever that was supposed to pick us up."

Now I'm feeling a teensy bit frantic. And to make things worse, the wind's up.

"My nose is feeling below zero," Nan says, joining me inside. "Keep looking for the phone."

I'm shining and feeling on the fourth wall when I touch something. The good news is I've found the phone. The bad news is the receiver comes off in my hand.

We're staring at each other like zombies when we hear a loud honk.

"It's them," Nan says. This time, the lights fill the tiny space and don't go away.

We run outside and see a large pickup truck waiting for us. A man in an Eskimo parka—much warmer-looking than mine—steps out of the cab and waves at us.

"Sorry I'm late, ladies. It's hard to gauge the road in winter—I ran into a slick spot and skidded into a ditch. Took a few minutes to rev my way out of it. Have you been waiting long?"

"Probably not," I say, "but it seemed like hours. Any-way, we're glad you're here."

We introduce ourselves and he tells us he's the manager Nan spoke to on the phone—Bud Granger. He tosses our packs into the back of the truck and squeezes all of us into the seat up front. Even though the truck's interior is roomy, it's a tight fit with three stuffed coats side by side.

"The phone didn't work," Nan tells him. "I don't know what we'd have done if you hadn't come."

"Wait for the next train, I guess."

He smiles, so I think that's supposed to be a joke. He sees we're not getting the humor, so he follows up by assuring us that there are houses in the area. I'm glad we didn't have to find out the hard way.

We ride for ten minutes or so in what seems to me to be pitch-darkness—I don't see one house, but I'm too relieved to argue. All I can think of is what we'd have done if he hadn't come.

"Did you ladies know we get dozens of Japanese newly-weds here? It's considered good luck to spend your honeymoon under the northern lights, and we've just built a big pavilion that's covered over with Plexiglas so you can see the lights without going outside."

I can't imagine what such a place would look like, but it's certainly not the log cabin I expected. When we pull up to the Old Gold Mine, the whole area is lit up for our arrival. Nan hasn't said a word—she's just gawking.

There's a huge central building that does indeed have a Plexiglas roof, and about half a city block away from it are separate little buildings. Each one looks like a modern motel room, only cut off from the other rooms by quite a distance. It's all fairly new, and Bud tells us the buildings are only five years old. He pulls up to the one where we'll be staying, and unlocks the door for us.

"This certainly isn't what I expected," Nan says. "So far away from civilization, I thought it'd be rugged."

"Oh no," Bud says. "This is deluxe. Did you want rugged?"

We look at each other.

"No, deluxe is fine," I say. "If it's heated, we'll take it."

"I like that *we'll take it*," Nan says—"as if we had a choice."

Bud takes us into the room, and it's indeed deluxe, in a Holiday Inn–ish sort of way. There's the standard everything—beige carpeting, Alaska posters on the walls, motel-style towels and bedspreads, and TV set. But definitely not standard is an enormous square hot tub in the bathroom.

"Wow, look at this," Nan says.

"Yep, that's for our honeymooners," Bud says, "for those Northern nights."

I'm thinking you could get four of his honeymooners into this thing. Not that I'm complaining—right now, a hot tub is exactly what I need to stop shivering.

"Come on over to the main building when you're ready," Bud tells us, "I'll fry you up a steak."

"What are your dinner hours?" Nan asks. "We don't want to sleep through it if we take a nap."

"There are no dinner hours. There're no guests. You're the only ones here."

"You're kidding—just us?" I say. "I knew tourists would be sparse, but I didn't realize they'd be nonexistent—I thought maybe there would be a few more like us."

"You're it. We've got restaurants a few miles from here, but they're only open in tourist season. I figured you'd want dinner and breakfast, so I made sure I had some extras on hand."

"Thanks," we both say at once. I guess there are lots of things we didn't even consider about this place.

"Why don't we give you a call when we're ready to come over?"

"No phone. I have a phone in the main building—none in the rooms. People like it that way. Privacy."

We race for the beds after Bud leaves, keeping our coats on until the room warms up to our satisfaction—meaning *hot.*

"I'm glad I'm not here alone," Nan says. "I'd be nervous about no phone in the room."

"Oh, I don't think there's any problem—we're not that far from that pavilion place."

"I guess."

chapter
26
....

"I'm starving," Nan says as we trudge over to dinner.
Again, my flashlight is indispensable, and I shudder to remember how casually I packed it for reading at night. We
have a dry lane from our room to the building, and the
snow of a few days ago has been neatly sliced through for
our path, obviously by machine. The banks are as high as
my chest, and I'm glad for my fleece-lined boots.

We open a massive wooden door to firelight, warmth,
and the odor of steak mixed with smoking logs. This must
be what's truly called a great room—dozens of wooden tables and benches, and on the log walls, artifacts and photos
of the original gold mine that was located here during
Alaska gold rush days. I like the room. It's authentic, unlike our weirdly suburban motel-type sleeping quarters.

"That's my dinner you smell," Bud says. "Yours'll be
ready when you want it. How about a drink? It'll all be
charged to your room."

He stands behind a massive curved bar, with some of the
bottles behind him looking as old as the place itself. Now
that he's out of his parka, we can see that he's maybe in his

forties, with a grizzly beard befitting his role as innkeeper of a former gold mine. He's even wearing a chunky gold-nugget ring to complete the look, and a striped full apron wrapped around a rather muscular body.

"I'm about to take a vacation in a few days during this downtime," he tells us. "I might have gone this week if you hadn't said you were coming.

"Since you called direct, I figured I'd take off next week instead. My help's all gone, but two guests is nothing to me. I can handle the cooking and setting up, and I don't mind the company."

He tells us we ought to try the brandy for a cold night, and we're only too happy to oblige, sitting on the bar stools and swiveling toward the fireplace for more warmth. We're certainly in no hurry, and he passes Nan some nuts with the brandy to tide her over.

"You owe me one," Nan whispers to me, and I agree. This is beyond special. We're grinning at each other, thinking that this scene is exactly what we'd hoped for. I'm so mellow by the time we finish our brandy that I've almost forgotten I'm hungry. But Nan hasn't—she gives Bud the signal and he starts our steaks. I don't expect a salad, but he has one ready, along with a baked potato and all the fixings.

"The coffee's the same recipe they used when this place was really cooking around 1917," Bud says. "The prospectors were all over this mine once the Tanana Valley Railroad was taken over by the railroad commission. Even earlier, we got some of the river trade to the gold fields."

"This coffee's not good, it's great," I tell Bud.

"You've got Ruby for life if she likes your coffee." Nan pours cream in hers, but I let myself down the real stuff, unadulterated.

I'm finally warm to the core for the first time after the food, coffee, and brandy by the fireplace.

"I'm getting sleepy," I say.

"I'm still a little sleepy, myself."

Bud hears my remark. "Oh, you have to stay awake for another hour. It's already eleven, and the light show's still to come."

"You mean the aurora borealis?" Nan asks.

"Sure. It's a big reason people come here in winter. The sky's not as reliable this early in November, but it's definitely possible you'll get a good show."

He leads us up some stairs to what he says used to be the roof of the building. It's been transformed into a domed area the size of an auditorium, with the whole sky visible from the inside. There's a balcony around the perimeter outside, too.

"You can take your cameras outside on the balcony for the best photos," he says. "But in case you don't like being out in below-zero weather, you can watch comfortably from inside. The temperature can reach minus forty degrees or more in the heart of winter."

It's amazing—I can't even imagine myself standing in that kind of cold. "But why did you make this area so large?" I say.

"We have big plans for these tours," Bud says. "We can have dinners for them here, and pallets for sleeping, too. Some of them like to sleep under the stars. The space makes it easy for us to partition the area into sleeping and eating sections."

Nan and I still can't quite believe what we're seeing— it's bizarre, especially since we're the only ones in this huge space.

Bud tells us that the Eskimos thought the multicolored streaks of light in the aurora borealis were caused by spirits of the dead playing ball games. The lights look like a modern laser show. Later in the season, the colors are deep and rich. For now, we'll see a more faded palette, mainly streaks of white and yellow light, with occasional rainbow colors.

"I hear they're doing scientific studies in Fairbanks," I say.

"Oh yes, they've studied the skies for years, but modern instruments have made it easier. The earth's magnetic field sends protons and electrons from the sun to the polar region, where they strike the atmosphere and glow, causing the northern lights."

Bud brings us more coffee and we sit on pallets on the floor to wait for midnight, when the skies will be at their best.

"More brandy in your coffee?"

We both turn that down. This is a once in a lifetime opportunity, and I'm not about to be sleepier than I already am when it starts.

"I'm turning in, then," Bud says. "Midnight's late for me, unless I have to stay up when the groups come. Do you remember how to get back to your cabin? Just go down the steps and out the front door. You'll see it straight down the slope."

"We left the inside and outside lights on," I tell him. "No problem."

"I'm glad he's gone, aren't you?" Nan says. "There's something about this vast silence out there that's almost sacred."

"I don't think we'll ever experience anything like this again. And to think it was sheer luck that he took us.

"Although I did sweeten the pot a bit over the phone, Nan. I told him we'd pay resort season rates if he'd let us in."

"Maybe he won't even put it on the books."

"In a way it makes it creepier," I say. "We left this phone number on our itinerary, but unless he's willing to say we've checked in if someone calls us, it's as if we don't exist here."

"And there's a good chance that if he's keeping the money off the books, he won't say we're here."

"So what, Nan? You'll have certainly been accountable enough in Kodiak and Fairbanks to satisfy your work ethic.

You're entitled to a night off the books once in a while. This *is* supposed to be partly vacation."

"More for you than for me, but don't get me wrong—I'm loving this."

"Let's go outside."

"What? Are you crazy? He said it was way below zero outside at night."

"I'll never be able to get good pictures under this dome. I've got to go outside if I want anything to turn out, so I might as well get set up for some practice shots. I don't even know what exposure to use."

"You'll get exposure, all right. I'll be carrying your frozen body back inside. Nothing doing."

"Okay, there's no reason to expect you to freeze your tail off so I can get good shots. I'll go out by myself."

"You mean we aren't going to watch the lights together? That's the fun of it."

"No, I promise I'll be right back in. I simply want to grab a few practice shots and then I can run out to take pictures when the lights are streaking by. I'll know what I'm doing by then, and I can do it faster."

"You have no idea what you're doing, and without longer exposures, you'll never get the photos you think you're going to get, anyway."

I'm out the door. It's no use arguing with Nan when she's like this, although she's probably right about the long exposures. But I'm not about to give her the satisfaction—and certainly not without trying.

Whoa. It's *cold*. Numbingly cold. I try a few shots of the sky, and I realize I can press the shutter with my gloves on—that's a relief. Now I see that I'll have to run in and out pretty quickly—it's hard to take more than a minute or two at a time out here, but it'll be enough. There are lots of stars out—just the right weather for the aurora, or so Bud said.

I run back in and sit on the floor beside Nan.

"How was it?"

"Breathtaking."

At that, we both crack up, since I find I hardly have any breath to get out that sentence.

"Okay, it was so cold you wouldn't believe it. And unfortunately, it did take my breath away pretty quickly. But I'm still taking pictures as soon as the lights begin."

"Be my guest—as if I could stop you."

"Of all our adventures together, this *beats it*. Can you imagine us here at the top of the world?"

It's now after midnight. We both lie down flat with our parkas still tight around us, boots, gloves, and hoods on, to wait for the northern lights. It doesn't take long.

The lights begin with a few streaks that look like shooting stars, then change into a display of pale multicolor—a low-key laser show. The colored streaks come and go, sometimes wheeling like a kaleidoscope.

"Eerie, isn't it?" Nan's looking through the transparent dome above us, which might be protected from the cold, but doesn't provide a clear view.

"Are you sure you won't go outside with me?" I say.

"Sorry. I don't want frostbite."

"You're not getting frostbite—trust me."

"Trust has nothing to do with it. I can see what's out there without your interpretation, and there's more cold than I've ever experienced."

"Your loss." I make another try with my camera—a fast dash outside before the mechanism freezes. I'm so intent on taking pictures, I don't even notice the cold until my face feels numb and I have to run back inside.

"The coffee's over there," Nan says.

Hot coffee never tasted this good. I join Nan on the floor now, and we both lie back and watch the somewhat filtered show.

I'm almost drifting off when Nan pushes my arm and whispers something.

"Can't hear you," I say.

She pushes again and I turn toward her. "Huh?"

"Don't you hear it?"

"I can hardly hear *you* with my parka hood tied this way."

"I've heard this bump two times. It's coming from over there."

She points toward a partially curtained area on the other side of the room—it looks like a storage area, and I can see chairs stacked up in some of the open spaces.

I remember vaguely that Bud's asleep somewhere in the building—his rooms are located downstairs on the same floor as the bar and restaurant.

"Maybe it's Bud moving something around downstairs," I say.

"I don't like it. I'm ready to go back to our cabin."

"Do you want me to check it out?"

"No. Let's just go. You've finished your picture taking. You still don't hear anything? There it goes."

This time I do hear a thump. But only a faint thump.

"It could be an animal, Nan."

She's on her feet already.

"I just meant a cat or something," I say. "I don't think the bears can get in here."

She's obviously not in the mood for my attempts at humor, since she's halfway across the room already, beckoning me to follow.

"Are we tiptoeing?" I ask when I catch up to her and notice a strange bounce to her walk. "I don't think you can tiptoe in snow boots, Nan."

She ignores me and breaks into a run when we hear yet another bumping noise. I'm out of excuses at this point, and decide she's right to want to get out of here. We race as fast down the stairs as our gear will allow, and Nan heads for the front door.

I grab her sleeve. "Hey, don't you think we should find Bud's apartment?"

"No, I just want to get back and lock us in."

Since I have no idea where Bud's quarters might be in relation to where we are now, I abandon that idea and follow Nan's wool scarf, flying in the wind behind her.

chapter
27
·······················

We've got that whole city block between the main building and our cottage to cover, but with the walks ice-free, we're able to move quickly. I look over my shoulder and see no one behind us, not that I actually expected to. The more pressing problem at the moment is that I can't breathe in this freezing air.

"Hey, slow down. I'm gasping—aren't you?"

"Yeah. Okay, I guess it's safe—there's no one here. I can't find the oxygen to pull into my lungs, Ruby. And it's so cold."

"This is beyond cold."

Although I can't say I'm particularly enjoying this, there's something about the experience that's once-in-a-lifetime. I can't quite take in the fact that I'm not that far from the Arctic Circle in the middle of the blackest night, under the aurora borealis, yet.

We manage to open the door without removing our gloves, a feat that takes two of us—me to steer the key toward the lock, and Nan to keep her hand under mine so there'll be a place for it to land in case we drop it. Neither of us wants to try picking a key up from the frozen ground with wool mitts.

This delicate task accomplished and the door opened, we stand still and breathe in the warmth of our room.

"I still think it was a cat," I say as we lock ourselves in with the dead bolt.

"I don't want to talk about that right now," Nan says. "I feel safe in here. I'll discuss it later, when we get in bed."

"Are you going to sleep in your clothes?"

"You mean my parka? I can't decide," she says.

"It's warm enough in here. I think we should take hot showers and put on our pajamas, socks, and a sweater."

"Uh-uh. I don't think I can do that. Just the thought of getting totally undressed makes me shiver."

"Okay, stay there, then. I'll take the first shower and you can see if I survive it."

I try the shower in the tub and it runs cold, so I stay dressed until I finally feel the heat from the spray. Not that much heat, actually. I chicken out and take a sponge bath standing outside the tub. It feels great to get clean, but I don't spend too much time at it. I pile on the socks, wool pj's, and sweater, and emerge from the bathroom without telling Nan about the sponge bath.

Not that it matters, because she's already in bed with the covers piled up to her chin. And I find out I didn't fool her, either.

"You didn't run the shower long enough to take a real one," she says. "And not a hair on your head is wet."

I glare at her, thinking that this close a friendship has its downside.

It's now two in the morning and neither of us is the least bit sleepy, even after the brandy. I guess the coffee offset it, or maybe pure excitement.

Then she comes at me with a zinger. "Ruby, do you think someone followed us up here?"

"No."

"Why?"

"It's ridiculous. I've never felt so alone in my life as I've felt here. Did it sink in that besides Bud, there's no one else in this whole resort?"

"What about those car headlights at the train stop—the ones that pulled away right before Bud drove up in his truck?"

"This place is a mile or more from the train stop. How do we know what's over the bend or whatever? That car could have been there to pick up someone who was supposed to get off the train, but didn't."

"I thought Bud implied that there were no houses close to us."

"I guess I wasn't listening. But no one in Alaska knows we're here—the only people we told are in Seattle and Eternal. You're scaring yourself because of a few noises back there."

"The people on the train knew we were getting off here."

"Yeah, but they didn't get off with us, did they?"

"Not that we know of."

"Nan, this is purely a recreational stop. No one besides Bud even knows our names."

"You told the fish supplier in Kodiak your name, and he gave it to his boss."

"And your name is known to everyone who attended the Forest Service hearing in Kodiak. What does that prove? That a disgruntled grievant is out to get you? And makes thumps in the middle of the night?"

"Okay. We've both ridiculed each other, so I guess we've neutralized the issue. I'll try to keep my fears to myself."

"No, that's definitely not what I'm after. If you're scared, you should tell me. And we both know you're going to, anyway. When did you ever keep anything important to yourself?"

"Never. I'm all right for now, though. Honest."

We roll over in our beds and it's not long before I hear a

faint snore coming from Nan's side of the room. I thought I'd be the one to fall asleep first, simply because I'd refreshed myself with the brief bath, while Nan stayed stuffed in the clothes she'd worn all day.

Instead, I'm still wide-awake. What a night. I know instinctively that I'll never spend another like it, and it makes me glad that this wasn't just another summer tourist junket. Someone in Arizona once told me that despite the fact that the place is a Mecca for winter visitors, the desert only comes into its own around the month of June, when the heat brings out the features most indigenous to it. Alaska's the same, and I sense that its essence is revealed on a subzero night in winter. Except for the fact that it's not snowing.

I turn over on my back and use this alone time to think about Nan's fears. I've been followed before, unfortunately, and I know what it feels like. I could even say that I have a natural intuition for it, and what I'm experiencing tonight is a much more peaceful, even fateful sense that we're in the right place at the right time.

chapter
28
....

I'm still awake, staring at the digital clock radio, which reads a depressing 4:30 A.M., when the red lighted numbers suddenly blank out. At first, I don't recognize the significance of this—my mind simply registers that the clock's broken. Since the rest of the room is pitch-dark and Nan's still sleeping peacefully, I decide to go with the flow and turn over under the blankets—maybe I can finally fall asleep. I still don't understand why insomnia has hit—it's not my style, but if I ignore it, maybe it'll go away.

It doesn't. I sit up and look at the clock, or where the clock face used to be, but I'm in total darkness. I make my way to the window and peek between the drapes.

I'm shocked. Our cottage is surrounded in white. It snowed more during the night, while I was lying here awake, I guess, although nothing is falling now. The snow is piled so high I feel as if our little room-house is floating in it. I can see an entrance light far up the lane at the main building, and in this darkness it's illuminating the ice far beyond what I'd imagine was its capacity—maybe because the snow is so reflective. I'm sure we're snowed in—it's high—halfway up the window already, which means it's up to my waist out there, at least.

I walk around to the other window by the front door, which is just off the path we walked last night to get back here from our sky viewing. The snow is even more visible, since it's in the direction of the main quarters. To my relief, I see snowshoe prints around our doorway. Bud must have tried to clear the path for us.

I'm feeling good enough about that to give the covers another try, so I practically dive into the blankets. Thank goodness for my thick wool socks. Nan's never going to believe I was awake all night long—maybe I can make up for some of the lost sleep in the next couple of hours.

I'm drowsy enough to fall into a half-dream of us chasing a thick orange column of salmon in a Kodiak Island stream, when I find myself sitting upright in bed. I hear our doorknob turning. I go over to the door, crack the window drape an inch, and see the knob turning—one way and then the other. But I can't see anyone. This is dopey. No one would be out on a night like this, except maybe Bud, and why would he be turning our doorknob? Since the dead bolt's latched, I'm not worried about the results, I'm just thinking this out, wondering if I'm asleep and dreaming.

I finally remember I have a flashlight, at the very moment I realize it'd be a bad idea to turn it on right now. To say we're pretty helpless here is an understatement, so why advertise that we're onto him—or them, or whatever. Maybe it's an animal. One that can turn knobs. Right.

Okay, before I wake up Nan, let's take stock.

One: It's getting cold in here.

Two: It's finally hitting me that our electricity is out.

Three: We're snowed in halfway up our windows.

Four: Someone's out there, and it's crazy to think it's Bud, who wouldn't be clearing walks at four in the morning.

Five: There's no telephone in the room.

How nice for Nan.

Well, here goes. I ease myself into her bed rather than have to raise my voice too loudly to wake her. Which will scare her less out of a deep sleep, being touched or hearing me whisper?

I go for the whisper.

"Nan? Hon—wake up."

Nothing.

I push her shoulder a tiny bit and she turns over, or tries to before bumping into me.

"Shhh." I try to look at her, have her look at me, shush her, and hold her shoulders to steady her, all at the same time. It finally works.

"What's wrong?"

"Whisper."

"Why are you over here?"

She *is* trying to whisper—I'll give her credit for that.

"Ruby, it's freezing in here."

"The electricity's out."

"Why are we whispering? And what do you mean the electricity's out?"

"I mean it's out. The clock doesn't work."

"Let's try the lamp by my bed."

I jump at that and throw myself between Nan and the lamp.

"No. Listen, I don't want to scare you, but I think there's someone out there."

I try to update her a little at a time that the doorknob's been rattling, there are footprints outside in the snow that piled up all night, and we have no phone service.

"Surely, those are Bud's prints."

"I don't think so."

"Why did we ever come somewhere with no phone in the room?"

"It's too late to worry about that now. If someone's after us, he could cut the line anyway. I should have brought a cell phone, but who knows if it would have worked here?"

"Let's wait until it's light outside and then go over to the main building."

"We've got four or five more hours until it's light in this place. I don't know how cold it will be in here by then with no heat."

One thing I know I'd better do, and that's to get dressed with everything piled on. I put on my Lands' End long johns, more sweaters and my thick pants, and finally my parka. And shoes.

Nan puts on her shoes, too, the only things she didn't sleep in. We pile the covers around us and sit on the bed again.

"Let's each take turns peering out the drape," I say. "There's enough light reflection on the snow to show the bare outline of a figure, if there is one."

"I want to look outside, anyway," Nan says. She stations herself slightly away from the window.

"OhmyGod, I can't believe the snow that's piled up, Ruby. This is unbelievable."

"Do you think we could make it to where Bud is?" I say.

"No. I'm not sure we could even move a few yards. We have no experience with this stuff. We've got to wait until it's light—surely Bud'll be looking for us by then. Didn't he say something about breakfast?"

"He mentioned his good pancakes."

Nan comes back and gets into bed. "Don't bother getting up," she says, "the chances of our seeing someone out there are nil."

"Maybe whoever rattled the doorknob left when he couldn't get in, thanks to the dead bolt," I say. "I'm realizing how risky it is not to have a phone in conditions like these. What if someone had a heart attack?"

"Let's try to turn on the light. What difference will it make?"

"I guess you're right."

She turns the switch but gets nothing. "It's my turn to be on duty now, Ruby. See if you can sleep."

I roll my eyes at the idea of sleeping with my boots, parka, and hood on, but I don't argue. I could certainly use the nap.

"I would suggest you read," I say, "but I think we should save the flashlight batteries in case we need to get out of here before dawn. Maybe we can both sleep."

I'm just dozing off when Nan starts up again.

"So, assuming a real live person who wasn't Bud appeared outside our door tonight, who was it?"

"Well," I say, "are you also connecting the thumps in the Plexiglas dome with this?"

"Yep. And whoever was in the other truck or car at the station stop, before Bud picked us up."

"Then I guess we have to go all the way back to the people in the train car with us, right?"

"Bear with me, Ruby. Suppose those fish distributors did have something to do with Herman's murder. I mean, we're not crazy, because *someone* knifed the man. That's not our imagination. And when you started asking questions all the way up here where they're headquartered, they could have wanted to scare you or shut you up. You got too close."

"So they sent someone to follow me on the train?"

"Yeah, to scare you or worse. And they did."

"And they came through these extreme conditions just to do this?"

"But it's only extreme to us, not them, Ruby. People living up here get around in this weather all the time—they know how to live with it. And this is only November—not even into real winter. Remember, it didn't even snow until tonight. And someone cut off this electricity—the main building still has lights out front."

"There could be a dozen reasons the electricity went off, Nan. We simply don't know. But I agree with you about people here getting around in bad weather. They're equipped for it. Can I try to get some sleep now? I've had none at all tonight, and I might need to at least function later today."

I guess she sees the logic in that, because she shuts up.

I hear nothing until I'm awakened by a loud knocking on the door.

chapter
29

....

We're both talking at once as we drag Bud inside, snow boots and all.

"Hold on. I can only hear one of you at a time."

Nan describes our night to him and he seems surprised enough to sit down on the side of the bed until she's finished.

While she's talking I pull the drapes aside and see that it's barely light, which means that it's already nine o'clock, at least. But I can see outside our doorway very clearly. I suddenly realize, though, that Bud's tracks might have obliterated any others.

"Maybe you're used to bumps in the night in your quarters," I say. "And I know, too, that the electricity in the rooms might sometimes go off. So I know you're not going to believe some of this."

"Don't be so sure," he says. "I saw tracks when I came down here just now. I thought maybe you'd opened your door and walked around outside. Before you tell me anything else, I'd feel better if you went with me back to the main building for breakfast—it's freezing in here. Let's go."

We start up the path—or what's left of the path—to

breakfast. Bud has broken through a lot of the snow for us, and we follow in his footsteps through waist-high piles. I look around and don't see any traces of the night's footprints, but he's seen them, and that's the important thing. Funny, but I'm feeling warmer just being able to trudge around, regardless of the fact that we're outside in the wind. Relief probably has something to do with my spirits, too.

We stomp off the snow and go inside as if magnetized by the aroma of coffee and something wonderful waiting on the grill—two piles of pancakes, more than either of us would usually be able to eat, but this morning, all bets are off. We peel away some of our top layers and enjoy the warmth of the fireplace. Bud has set a small table by the fire for us and waits on us as we sit, zombielike, staring at the flames. We both wolf down pancakes, syrup, and lots and lots of that great black coffee.

Nan's slumped in her chair. "I feel like I'm in a waking dream," she says. "All this cold keeps you so drowsy."

"Not to mention the interrupted sleep last night," I say.

Bud's smart enough to be quiet until we eat, and for a long time, the only sounds we hear are the logs spitting in the fire. My hands and face still feel numb in the warmth of the room, and I've lost all track of time, so I ask.

"It's ten," Bud says. "Since it'll get dark by midafternoon, we try to cram a lot in during the daylight hours. I have a delivery of supplies coming out here today, and after I help unload them, I'll drive the two of you to your Fairbanks hotel like we arranged. I'll need enough time to get back here before dark."

He hasn't brought up the subject of our middle-of-the-night scare, and I want to tell him we're ready to talk about it.

"I think you need some background to last night, Bud."

I'm interrupted when a horn honks outside.

"You okay with the food?" he says. "Plenty of coffee in

the pot. I'll be at the loading dock. This won't take too long."

We assure him we're fine, and as soon as he goes out the back door, Nan glares at me.

"You weren't thinking of spilling that whole thing to him about Herman's murder without checking with me first, were you?"

"Well, I guess I was ready to say *something*, but you could have always stopped me—you've never been shy before."

"It's not a question of being shy—it would have been hard to have tried to change the subject."

"Okay, I'm sorry."

"I'm just wary of how far back you were going to go with Bud, Ruby. We don't know this guy, and I think we should decide how much we'd tell the authorities if it came to that, and not tell Bud any more. I'd like to put this behind us until we get out of here and to my Fairbanks hearing—we're in no condition to reason well—at least, I'm not."

"We'll never see him again, Nan. We owe it to ourselves to see what he thinks of those footprints. Once we leave here, any conversations will be by phone and will be too difficult to gauge. I've thought about this, and in my opinion, there's no way he could be responsible for what happened last night."

"I don't believe he is, either, but we're not in any state to work it out. My idea is to let him talk. Let's ask him questions and see if he has any thoughts about what happened."

We're both too curious to stay away from the loading dock, so we head in the direction of the back door and look out one of the windows. Bud sees us and waves, pointing us out to the driver, who gives a wave, too. They're loading a dolly with cardboard boxes—there don't seem to be too many supplies.

We go back in by the fire and have to wait only a few minutes for Bud.

"Aren't you freezing?" I say.

"It doesn't even bother me," he says. "This isn't real winter for us yet. The next few months are the cold ones."

I realize we don't have that much daylight to waste, so I think about changing the subject. Before I can open my mouth, Nan starts asking the questions. I guess it *was* her idea.

"Bud, who in the world could have tried to open our door last night? No sane person would be out in that weather."

"We've only had a few robberies out here," he says, "but Alaska's no different than any other place these days. The weather wasn't that bad, and it wouldn't have stopped anyone who wasn't a tourist. I'm guessing it might have been someone wanting to loot the empty rooms in winter. It's never happened, but that's not to say it couldn't. Maybe some teenagers."

"You mean they thought it was empty?"

"Well, you didn't leave any prints when you went to bed—you said it wasn't snowing yet. Maybe it looked unoccupied to them."

"Do you ever hear noises late at night in the big observation room?" I ask.

"I'm not up there by myself at that time of night. And when crowds are here, I couldn't hear noises anyway."

"But who would cut the electricity off in the room?"

"That could have been a fluke. Something you plugged in?"

"If we'd plugged something in," I say, "the power would have gone out right away. I was watching the digital clock from bed when it stopped."

"Then I don't know. I do realize it wasn't the greatest idea to let two guests stay in these cottages with no one else in the place. I'm not going to do it again, and I don't think I should charge you."

"No," we both say, "let us pay."

"You've been great," Nan says, "and you even cooked for us."

When we've piled in the truck later with all our gear, Bud asks us if we got a good light show. We promise to send him my pictures of him and the aurora if they turn out.

"Don't be surprised if they don't," he says. "People use special equipment to photograph the aurora. They've done lots of research on it at the UAF, the University of Alaska at Fairbanks, up on the bluff. They show a great movie of it at the museum on campus."

When he finally pulls up at our downtown hotel, I'm ready for the usual good-byes, but Nan's still curious.

"Bud, are you going to report the tampering of the room to the police?"

"What can I say to them?" he says. "Nobody actually broke in. They're not going to be interested to hear that the electricity went out, are they?"

Nan's hearing in Fairbanks turns out to be less stressful and more social than in Kodiak—we find ourselves enjoying the company of her colleagues and seeing the sights with them.

We don't have a good opportunity to dwell on the northern lights incident until we're taking off for Seattle from the Fairbanks airport. I'm personally relieved to see that we're headed toward more sunlight. I'd have never believed that flying on our way to Washington State in bleak November would represent a step in that direction, but it does.

Seattle may be dark at this season, but that depends on what you're comparing it with—and to me, it also means we're that much closer to the bright Texas skies of the Sunbelt. I'm not sure I could survive psychologically through those endless winter nights in Alaska, despite the beautiful snow scenes and the promise of the long days of summer.

Nan's take on our experience at the gold mine is that the whole night was so surreal she's not sure now that anything threatening really happened.

"How can you say that?" I say. "I'm here to tell you it happened."

"But that's what I mean," she says. "You were awake most of the night—I wasn't. You heard the doorknob rattle—I didn't. The clock went out while I was asleep. When I think about it now, it seems like a dream."

"You're not—"

"No, Ruby. Absolutely not. I'm not doubting for a minute that it all took place. I'm just saying it makes it hard for me to re-create the events, or to come to some conclusion about them. I don't know what to think."

"But you were the one who made me pack up and leave the observation room when you heard the noises."

"I know I did, but I could also have been anxious about nothing."

"How about the footprints, Nan?"

"Real, but as Bud said, there's nothing you could nail down and actually show the police. It's not as if they broke in."

"So what are you saying?"

"That we should probably forget it, Ruby, and be glad nothing worse happened. When we get home, it's going to seem like part of Alaska—far away and hard to reach."

chapter
30
....

I'm hoping for Ed at the Austin airport. What I get is Essie Sue, Kevin, the twins, and two ice coolers.

"We brought the coolers for your salmon," Essie Sue says.

"You're kidding. You think I carried the Bar Mitzvah food on the plane?"

"I thought you might have samples."

The woman really does think I made this trip for her benefit, and that the state of Alaska is one big Zabar's of the North.

"I'm disappointed, Ruby. I wanted to audition the fish."

"You can audition the dried and smoked kind—they're flat for packing and make great souvenirs."

"But they're not lox, right?"

"Right."

"What about the orders? Did you put in a reservation with the distributor?"

"No, their main office was in Seattle, and all I saw was the airport on my way to Alaska."

"So what good were you?"

I ignore this. I'm still half looking around for Ed, hoping he'll be here to pick me up, but I don't mention it. I'll get my excuses from him, not from Essie Sue.

"Your boyfriend Ed had a work assignment and couldn't come," Kevin says. "He said to tell you he was really sorry, but that he'll be back in two days. So Essie Sue said she'd pick you up, so she could get your salmon samples."

Just what I needed to hear, but I can't deal with it now—I have a more pressing worry. After thanking Essie Sue for driving up to Austin, I take Kevin aside and ask about my house.

"It's not a disaster zone, is it? I don't think I could face that."

"No, I left it in tiptop condition. Essie Sue even came over to check it out. Briefly."

"How briefly?"

"I swear. It's fine, Ruby."

Only now do I feel safe enough to speak to the twins directly.

"I brought you some Eskimo tools, guys, but only if you were careful in my house. Were you?"

"Oh, yeah."

Lester pokes Larry and smirks. I don't like the smirk.

"What's wrong?"

"Nothing. The rabbi said we couldn't wreck anything, and we didn't."

I don't like their body language, either.

"Essie Sue, did anything happen while I was gone?"

"Of course not, Ruby. I told you Lester and Larry would be perfect gentlemen. I checked."

"You slept in the guest room, right?"

They nod *yes.*

"And you slept on the sofa bed I unfolded in the living room, Kevin?"

"You were right—it's comfortable. I slept okay."

"So let's go, then. I'm anxious to pick up Oy Vay—I want her home tonight."

"They're bringing her over for you," Essie Sue says, "so we can go straight home."

There are times when a big Lincoln really does the job, and this is one of them. We ride in style down the highway to Eternal, and I even doze a bit in the car. I can relax since Kevin's in the backseat with the kids.

"As a man I should be in front. I'm bigger," he says, but Essie Sue pays no attention.

"Any news on what happened to Herman?" I ask Essie Sue.

"He's dead. What else could happen to him?"

Oy. "Don't be so literal, Essie Sue—are they any closer to solving the murder?"

"Lieutenant Lundy asked me some more questions, but aside from that, I haven't heard anything. I think the daughter is getting restless. She told me she was ready to go to the papers."

"The papers? What does she have to say that she hasn't said already?"

"I have no idea."

I keep waiting for Essie Sue or Kevin to ask about my trip. Zilch. Hard to believe if you didn't know them.

I'm holding my breath as we drive up Watermelon Lane, but I'm pleased to see that my house is still standing and looks the same as when I left. Oy Vay's waiting in the backyard, and jumps all over me. Maybe I should stick to dogs—at least one creature is thrilled I'm home.

I grab my bags, hoping for some help, but none is forthcoming. This might be for the best, since I can wave the four of them off as soon as the trunk is closed. I want to be alone in the house to settle in. I say good-bye and thank you again, and put my key in the lock as I hear them drive away.

"Can we see what you brought us?"

To say I'm startled would be a major understatement—
my nerves are on edge from the events of the trip, anyway,
and this shock has me literally jumping forward and almost
stumbling across the threshold.

Lester and Larry are right behind me.

"Can you unpack our souvenirs here, Ruby?" *Now*
Lester decides to help with the bags, or rather, to try unzip-
ping my backpack.

"Why are you here?" I'm still in shock.

"We're sleeping here with you. Remember?"

"You mean they just left you here?"

They shrug. "We're having special tutoring this week
before school starts," Larry says.

"Essie Sue's supposed to take care of you in the day-
time," I say, "and besides, I'm only having you on weekends."

This is beyond *chutzpah*, and now I can see the planning
behind the airport pickup. I'm always thinking nothing
else can surprise me.

"Come on in, boys, and I'll give you a drink while I call
Essie Sue."

"Oh, we know where everything is," Lester says. "The
rabbi said we could have the run of the refrigerator if we
wouldn't bother him when he was watching TV."

I go to the refrigerator and see that all the cartons of soft
drinks I had in the back pantry are now stacked on the
shelves. The freezer's empty.

"He said we could eat the ice cream and anything else
we could find."

Just for the hell of it, I open the pantry and see most of
those shelves are also bare, but the food's the least of it. On
the surface, my kitchen looks the same, but there's something strange about it. Dish towels and newspapers are
spread out all over the place. I lift only one of the towels—
with the same gingerly touch I'd use to open a public
bathroom stall. This one conceals empty cereal boxes, un-

washed bowls, glasses, and plates. I don't want to know yet what else is hidden.

"We made it all neat for when Cousin Essie Sue came over. She looked in the kitchen and said it was fine."

They look up at me with solemn faces, but it doesn't take much staring on my part before they're holding in the laughs, looking as if they're ready to burst.

"And you thought this would fool me?"

"No, but we thought it would fool Cousin Essie Sue. We figured we could help you later."

"Did the rabbi help you clean up?"

"No," Larry says, "he told us he'd give us five dollars each if we did it in thirty minutes before she came over to take us to the airport. We did it, too." They high-five.

"So what other surprises do you have for me?" I say as I run upstairs. Thank God I locked my bedroom.

The guest room's a total mess, with unmade beds and the boys' clothes all over the place, but it's all in one piece, and no lamps are broken. No surprises here—I would have expected it, but the kitchen's a whole other thing.

"We short-sheeted the rabbi's bed one night," Lester says, "but he said he'd forgive us if we didn't bother him anymore."

I go back down to look at the living room, which is covered also—in this case, with afghans and blankets. I peek under, and see everything from pop cans to Chee•tos bags to tennis balls.

"Can we have our presents?"

"Another day, after I get unpacked. Right now, stay where you are."

"How about TV?"

"Sit down right in front of it and don't go anywhere. Okay?"

Essie Sue's answering machine is on. I start to leave a message when I get a better idea.

"Come on, boys—we're going for a ride."

I pack them into the backseat of my car, which is thankfully safe in my locked garage, and head for the Margolises'.

I see her peering through the curtains in her upstairs window, so I ring the bell nonstop until she answers.

"Go on in, boys," I say, "I want to talk to your cousin."

She looks horrified as they run past her into the entrance hall.

"No, Larry and Lester. Go right onto the deck in back." She runs to make sure they do.

I follow her inside and wait until she returns.

"Ruby, I'm getting ready to make Hal's dinner now. You're going to have to take the twins back to your house. You know our agreement."

"Explain our agreement to me, Essie Sue."

"You're supposed to let the kids sleep there when they're in town."

"Wrong. Only on the weekends when they're up here for classes. And even then, it's only to sleep—the rest of the time, they're yours."

"Well, that's not what they're used to. When you were away—"

"Did you even look at what happened at my house while I was away?"

"Yes, it looked fine."

"We're driving back there right now, and this time, you're looking *under* the towels."

"I have to fix dinner, and I didn't prepare for the boys."

"Hal's home, and he can take the kids out. Let's go."

I head for the den to find Hal, when she suddenly gets the idea I mean business.

"Okay," she says, "I'll go speak to Hal myself. Maybe he can amuse them for a few minutes, and then I can explain to you why they should stay at your house tonight. You're just tired, Ruby. You owe me. After all, I was nice enough to drive all the way to Austin to get you."

"But what did it cost me, Essie Sue? Believe me, a cab-driver wouldn't have demanded any deals."

Now I have another gripe with Ed—why couldn't he have saved me all this? And why hasn't he called? Oh. One good explanation could be that I haven't checked my messages at home. Yet another reason to finish this standoff with Essie Sue.

She follows me home and I wait at the front door until she parks, so that we can view the debacle together.

"I didn't have a lot of time to check things out," she says. "You didn't want me to be late for the airport, did you?"

"Since you're already making excuses, I'm assuming you have some idea of what I walked into," I say.

"No, I never saw it."

"Okay, then you'll see it now."

I strip all the afghans off the living room floor and sofa. Then I lead her into the kitchen and do the same thing with the towels covering all the garbage on the floor and counters. I don't bother with the guest room, because I expected the boys to mess up their own room—although I'd hoped Kevin might make them clean it up before I got home.

Since this is the woman who doesn't allow a speck of dirt to contaminate her premises, I'm hoping the shock value alone will move her. Her face pales, but I can tell from her look that she's preparing some sort of quick defense.

"Don't even think of it," I say. "Don't dare tell me boys will be boys. I just want to know what you're going to do about this."

"It's the rabbi's fault—he was supposed to supervise them. He'll have to make them clean it up."

"Uh-uh. I want a cleaning service in here tomorrow morning. I'll let you worry about the boys' training on your own."

I should have known she'd be relieved at a solution that merely required a phone call and a credit card.

"That's fine, Ruby. I'll call them. So we're even?"

"Not on your life. I'll still honor our agreement to let them sleep over here on Bar Mitzvah class weekends. But they're yours for these special sessions with Kevin—that's not part of the bargain. Once I'm in charge of them at my own house, messes like this won't be a problem. Larry, Lester, and I will have an understanding. Big time."

"But I told you that Hal can't stand to have them around because of his heart problems."

"Not to mention your own palpitations when your house becomes Three Mile Island, but that's between you and the boys."

"But this is giving me no advance warning. . . ."

"Not to be inhospitable, Essie Sue, but I'm retreating upstairs to my locked bedroom. I'll expect the cleaners first thing in the morning. As for now, I'm wiped."

Oy Vay comes in from the backyard and helps me escort our guest to the door. Although she waits patiently while I lock the dead bolt, I have to put her leash on as soon as she sniffs the junk food court in the living room.

"Sorry, baby," I say, "I know this would make quite a playground, but it's off limits. I can only take so much in one day."

chapter
31

....

E-mail from: Ruby
To: Nan
Subject: *Safe, but Not Sound*

Dropping a line as I told you I would, to let you know I'm home okay. I've never been so glad to be in this bed, fresh from the shower and luxuriating on clean sheets. And my only companion is Oy Vay, in case you were wondering. Ed was out of town and couldn't pick me up.

The Levee twins wrecked my house under Kevin's careful supervision, but I'll go into that later—I can't deal with it now.

I have messages on my answering machine from Paul Lundy, Ed, and Herman's daughter Rose, among countless others you wouldn't be interested in. I haven't gotten back to anyone.

Plus, I have a stack of e-mail messages that, alone, could keep me off the computer for months if I gave in to my true feelings and decided to procrastinate. The problem with my having been online ten years before everyone else is that there's now this huge lag between my interest and theirs. The same e-mail that's so new and intriguing to my friends is now a colossal chore for me. Not to mention the business e-mails.

As you can see, this is just coming-home fatigue tonight—sorry for the complaining.

I do want to run something by you, though. Do you have time tonight, or are you already asleep?

....

E-mail from: Nan
To: Ruby
Subject: *I'm Up*

Go for it. I slept a bit, but now I'm awake, and I wanted to make sure I heard from you when you got home.

I'm groaning for you—walking in on a trashed house—let me know more.

And of course I want to hear your thoughts on what happened to us at the gold mine place.

....

E-mail from: Ruby
To: Nan
Subject: *Making a Possible Mountain out of a Possible Molehill*

Okay, here goes. I know we disagree about what in the hell to think about the night we were snowed in, and there's certainly plenty of room for different interpretations of those events. I respect your good sense enough to concede you might be right. But when something's nagging at me, I have to respect that, too.

As annoyed as I am with Ed, I'm going to lay this all on him and see what his take is. To me, this is the story he *didn't* have before, when Herman first asked him to investigate the lox distributors. I don't blame him for opting out of that one, but now, unfortunately, Herman, who initiated this, is a murder victim. Even if nothing comes of it, I'll bet anything Ed can persuade his editors to let him loose on this. He has a great nose, and he'll tell me if anything that happened when I was in Kodiak and outside Fairbanks is simply catastrophizing on my part.

And should I tell Paul? If so, when? Before I talk to Ed? I can't forget this is also a police investigation.

••

E-mail from: Nan
To: Ruby
Subject: *Your Nose Is Good, Too*

I trust your take, also. Tell 'em both. But first, why don't you let them do the talking—they're the ones who left messages. Maybe whatever they have to say can help you decide how to go.

Meanwhile, I wanted to say I thought Alaska was incredible, didn't you? The beauty of visiting there in the wintertime was a bonus we could have so easily missed as tourists only. We'll never forget this.

••

E-mail from: Ruby
To: Nan
Subject: *Our Trip*

No, we'll never forget. I'm going to bed now to dream about stars and snow. And salmon.

chapter
32
....

Ed and I are surface-diving at Barton Springs, on one of those unbelievable early December Sundays that make our winters here so worthwhile. Last night we had dinner at Chuy's, his favorite Mexican restaurant in Austin, and stayed overnight at a downtown bed-and-breakfast. Essie Sue actually agreed to sleep with the twins at my house in Eternal so that I could have this weekend with Ed. She volunteered Kevin to baby-sit, but he's forbidden to cross my threshold since his botched attempt at discipline earlier last month.

In Austin and Eternal, no one quite puts away shorts for the winter—you never know when the temperature will pop up to 75 or higher. Today it's 80 degrees outside, and the famed natural aquifer waters of Barton Springs remain at 68 degrees, their year-round temperature. To dive into 68-degree water on a summer day when the air temperature's soaring is one thing, but it's also a joy to snorkel on a day like this, and the place is full of people swimming and picnicking on the hillsides.

"I'll race you to the shallow end," Ed says, and I take

him up on it. The pool is a thousand feet—more than three football fields long—and we've been watching fish and salamanders all morning. I love the thought that native peoples were enjoying these waters over ten thousand years ago just as we are today. It's an amazing place.

Ed wins—he's a faster swimmer than I am—and we loll with the little kids on the slippery rocks of the shallow end, soaking in the sun. It's been a good reunion, and I don't need convincing that our feelings are mutual on the subject of missing each other. Our time together has made that obvious.

"Can you believe it could possibly be thirty below now in Fairbanks?" I say. I've told him all about our adventure at the gold mine site, my conversation with the fish distributor in Kodiak, and the mysterious truck that flashed its lights at us while we were stranded at that remote train shelter.

"I don't know," he says now when I bring it up again. "A lot of what you experienced could be smoke and mirrors, even though it frightened you at the time."

I'd be put off by his words if I hadn't seen that keen look in his eyes that he only gets when he's sizing up a story. I know him well enough by now not to underestimate that look.

"You thought Herman was an interesting character even before he was murdered," I say. "Now it's a different matter entirely. Maybe the story's got legs."

Ed's enough of a professional that I don't waste a lot of energy on making my point—he'll either go for it or he won't, and a lot will depend on the case he can make to his editors. If he believes in it enough, I think his track record is such that he could persuade them. I could tell he wasn't originally all that convinced by Herman's suspicions. It could be that the murder will keep him investigating.

I'm prepared to change the subject, but he surprises me.

"Have you spoken to Paul Lundy yet about your trip?" he says.

"No, I had too much to catch up on with work and at the bakery. I also wanted to wait until I told you."

"Why don't you see what information he can give you about how the case is going, and what his reaction is to the Alaska stuff?" he says. "I have my reasons for not wanting to talk to him at this point, but I'd be interested in coming in through the back door if you want to take the lead. Interested?"

"Of course I'm interested. I owe it to him to report anything from the distributors, anyway," I say. "That would seem to relate to the investigation, and as far as I've heard, the case is still ongoing."

"Which probably means they've gotten nowhere," he says.

"I think before I call Paul, I'll speak to Herman's daughter, Rose," I say. "She's keeping tabs on everything, and she left a message on my answering machine when I was away. We're still playing phone tag."

When Ed finally has to say good-bye, I try to ward off that empty feeling I always get in the pit of my stomach by driving home via Rose's house. I see her car parked in the driveway and take a chance that I won't be disturbing her on a Sunday. Since we're not exactly close friends, I feel a bit awkward dropping in, but while I'm sitting in my car deciding whether to ring the bell or drive off, she comes out on the porch with a watering can.

"Ruby, is that you?"

I guess I don't have a choice now.

"It's me. I was debating with myself whether to get out of the car or not—when I realized this was the weekend, it seemed rather inconsiderate to visit without calling."

"You're welcome anytime—come on in—Ray's with his bowling team."

We sit on the porch and Rose brings me a glass of iced tea. She's very curious about Alaska, and I find myself talking about the trip for the better part of a half hour. All the time I'm yakking, my mind is censoring the conversation. I hate myself when I do this. I'll throw myself into a situation impulsively—like this sudden visit—and then realize I've made no plans as to how to proceed.

I'd wanted to ask Rose about developments in the case, but it didn't even occur to me that I'd end up talking about Alaska. I have no intention of frightening her with my spooky tales of footprints in the snow when she's on edge already. But I do feel I should tell her I spoke to the man in Kodiak.

She reacts to that mildly enough, which is a relief.

"So do you think the company will follow up on your visit and look into my father's charges? I know it would have given him some satisfaction."

We're both blinking back tears at this. I'm remembering that day we found him, and I try to recover by concentrating on my iced tea.

"We don't know what your father's charges include—if the whole company's involved, my visit might not do any good at all." And could have done harm, but I don't burden her with that.

As if she knows my mind's not on Alaska, Rose steers the conversation back to Eternal, where I wanted to focus in the first place.

"The police haven't been in close touch with me while you were gone," she says, "so I figured nothing's happening with the investigation."

"Oh, I'm sure they're working on it."

"Then could you ask, yourself, now that you're back? You and Lieutenant Lundy seem to be friends, and maybe he'd fill you in as to any new leads."

"Sure. I was going to call him anyway, but I don't think you should hesitate to contact him for information from time to time. If you're not an interested party, I don't know who would be."

"They always seem so preoccupied over there—I feel as if I'm taking up their time."

"So what? That's their job. And it's my feeling that it's the *noodges* who get the attention with busy people. Go for it."

My muscles are starting to ache from the long swim at the springs this morning, and I'm ready to take off when I think of something I've forgotten to ask.

"Did you ever read those papers in Yiddish that you found in Herman's house?"

"Oh, you mean the ones I gave our cousin to translate? He procrastinates a lot, and I wouldn't say he's the brightest man I ever knew. But he does speak and read Yiddish. I'll call and hurry him up. If he hasn't started, it's going to take him a while."

"Maybe you can transcribe for him. With you beside him, he's more likely to stay on track."

Rose walks me out to the car and assures me that my drop-in wasn't an intrusion. What a lovely woman.

As I get in the car, I can't help one final *noodge*.

"Why don't you call your cousin today, Rose?"

chapter
33

··························

Two down, one to go. So much for my belated lox re-
ports. I've decided to tell Essie Sue and Kevin nothing,
Rose a bit more, Ed everything, and Paul as much as I can
without risking a warning to stop investigating.

I waited until after the late December holiday season
and the New Year, too, before trying to see Paul. I've
snagged him for lunch, since it's a Monday and his entire
day's schedule is filled except for the noon hour.

"You've got to eat," I say. "Right?"

"Usually," he says, digging into his barbecue chicken
plate. "How come you didn't insist on eating at the bakery?"

I brush that off, but actually, there are lots of reasons.
Essie Sue and Kevin are there often, as is Rose, plus people
from the Temple who drop by my table to talk. Today I
wanted Paul's undivided attention. By lunching in an out-
of-the-way place, I've avoided having to make a bunch of
explanations about our meeting, and I've escaped the
dreary atmosphere at the police station. Lunch on a paper
towel in the interrogation room is not my idea of culinary
pleasure.

Neither is this place, come to think of it, but it'll do. The barbecue used to be a lot better two owners ago, when the luncheonette had a hotshot cook. I thought I'd bring Paul here to try the new chef's wares, but I hadn't realized they'd hired two cooks since the original hotshot. Not a good sign. I settle for a side salad with thoughts of blueberry cobbler later. À la mode.

"I gather this isn't just a friendly lunch," Paul says, leaving me to explain myself.

"Why couldn't it be?" I ask. "You never used to be so snippy about meeting me."

"I know you, remember? You've got that hungry look in your eyes—the one that doesn't just mean friendly lunch."

"Could be I'm only hungry. Yum."

Paul puts down his fork. "Sorry, Ruby, but the barbecue's not that good, and you know it. And how long has it been since we had anything resembling a social meeting?"

Uh-oh. Shades of Ed Levinger are creeping in here, at a time when they're most unwelcome. This isn't the atmosphere I intended to set up, so I'd better get to the point fast.

"Okay, so you do know me all too well. I'm asking for your take on something I did a bit rashly on my vacation. I dropped into the Acme Jobbers outlet in Kodiak and might have overexposed myself."

"That was smart. With the Guenther murder unsolved, you barged into the den of possible thieves and told them what, exactly?"

"That Herman had been killed and that the bakery wanted to deal directly with their company for a special salmon order."

"You had to mention the murder?"

"Look, it's a fact, and I wanted to be up front about it. I didn't want them to believe I was baiting them. Besides, this was all I could think of on the spur of the moment. I'd really wanted an excuse to look the place over, but it was the wrong season and there wasn't much to see. I had to find some excuse to be there."

"You're not finished, are you?"

"Not exactly."

"That look's still on your face."

"Forget the look—can't you manage to eat and listen without staring me down?" Paul can really be annoying when he thinks he has the upper hand. I try to keep going and ignore the attitude.

"I got a scare when we left Kodiak and went north of Anchorage to a fairly isolated resort."

He's patient enough when I describe the train ride and losing electricity in the cottage, but his nose twitches when he hears about the doorknob rattling and the unexplained footprints outside.

"Bud Granger, the innkeeper, couldn't explain the footprints, since we told him they weren't ours, and they weren't his, either. I saw them before he arrived, and he got a good look at them, too, when he shoveled a path to our door in the morning."

"What *did* he think?"

"He said it could have been kids wanting to loot the empty cottages, but he didn't seem all that convinced. I don't believe he knew any more than we did."

Paul's laid down his fork in the middle of the unfinished plate. If he's not eating, I know he's upset.

"You've put yourself in danger again, and it was so unnecessary, Ruby. You didn't have to go chasing these people down."

I ignore the danger part—there are plenty of other distractions.

"Paul, it's very difficult for me to believe the distributors had someone follow us in that heavy snow."

"Why? Because it's Alaska? You've already told me November's easy to deal with there. Maybe the snow doesn't mean the same thing to them that it does to you."

"If you're right, then Bud's idea of the kids' looting isn't any less realistic than that someone followed us."

"Did you want my input on this or not? If you have it all resolved, why are you sitting here with me?"

"Sorry. So why would they do this?"

"To scare you off. It worked, didn't it?"

"Well, I guess it did, although I wasn't planning to do any other investigating, anyway."

"But they didn't know that. It could have been a warning."

"Then I guess we were lucky they didn't break in."

"Nah. As you describe it, the cottage was so isolated they could have done whatever they wanted. Trust me, if someone wanted to bust in that door, he could have done it. As well as grab the two of you at the train stop. This was a scare."

"It seems unlikely that they'd even get organized that fast after I appeared at the fish plant."

"How many tourist hotels are there in downtown Kodiak, Ruby? They wouldn't have had to follow you at all—you'd already given them your name. Making a few phone calls could have located you, and from there, going up on the train with you was easy. I'm sure they were also curious as to what you were up to next. They could check on you and warn you off at the same time."

"So one of those people lolling at the back of the railcar could have been my tail?"

"It's as good an explanation as any."

"Has anything happened while I've been gone that could possibly dovetail with this scenario? I'm not saying I believe it, but I'm curious."

"Nope. We've got zilch, Ruby. No fingerprints on the knife in Guenther's back, no signs of struggle, no entrance or exit residue."

"Maybe that's why you're so ready to believe my scare was connected—you haven't got anything else."

He actually snickers at that, and goes for the coleslaw again. "Yeah, you can see how desperate I am."

"That's the first kind look I've had from you all day."

"It wasn't that kindly. I'm still mad at you for putting yourself at risk. You didn't even ask me first."

"I'd promised Essie Sue to set up a big catering order for the Bar Mitzvah. It didn't seem that risky to me."

"Nope, you're not that naïve. You wanted to see what would happen."

"So what do we do?"

"About your adventure? Nothing. I have a few things to think about as a result, but unless I have more, I have nothing on these people."

We dip into the warm cobbler the waitress has put down in front of us—so warm that it's melting the homemade vanilla ice cream. For a couple of minutes we're lost in it.

"So how's your friend the journalist?"

The question seems more straightforward than his usual references to Ed—maybe the syrupy blueberries have momentarily mellowed him.

"Funny you should ask. I told Ed that, unfortunately, Herman's story seems a lot more interesting now that he's a murder victim and not merely a dissatisfied customer of some fish vendors."

"Always stirring the pot, huh, Ruby?"

"I guess you could say that."

"This might surprise you, but some publicity might be exactly what this case needs."

"You'd cooperate with him? Could I tell him that? Remember, he has to convince his paper first—I figure he'll need some ammunition."

"Let me check it out with a couple of people first. I'll give you a call."

"Why not give Ed a call, instead?"

"I'll give you a call."

My gut tells me not to push it. If they both want to make me the go-between, why not? I suppose this isn't the time to say what I'm really thinking, which is that this is such a guy thing, it's pathetic.

chapter
34

····················

It's not until I've leafed halfway through the treasure trove Rose has brought me that I'm sorry I've asked her to meet me here at The Hot Bagel. Although it's true that our morning breakfast crowd has gone and even the earliest lunchers aren't here yet, I keep watching the door. Rose's hands are shaking as she spreads the contents of the ancient little wooden chest across my side of the bakery's most out-of-the-way corner table near the kitchen.

Milt, who knows me well enough to stay at a distance when I have a certain look in my eyes, provides just the right touch of nurturing. He pours Rose a cup of Columbian coffee to go with the unbuttered poppy seed bagel she's ordered, being careful not to bring the pot anywhere near my side of the table where it might spill.

I whisper something to him that hopefully appears innocuous to Rose, but what I'm really telling him is to keep an eye on that door—I don't want any surprises. I've been surprised enough this morning by what's in front of me.

Rose called and woke me at seven this morning to tell me she'd finally been invited to her cousin's last night to pick up his translation of Herman's letters. When he gave her the carefully handwritten sheets of yellow legal paper converting the words into English from Yiddish, he also handed her the small wooden chest I'm examining now.

"The letters I gave my cousin," she tells me between bites, "reminded him of more mementos my father had asked him to keep for him years ago. My cousin's house is so cluttered, he'd forgotten all about them until he was reminded by the content of the materials he was translating."

Everything in my hands is obviously prewar, or at least *old*. There are postcards, photos, and letters, musty but in good shape.

"Look at these," Rose says. "There are so many of this young woman and my father."

A pretty blonde stands beside a young Herman—they're standing in some sort of village square, holding hands. The girl looks no more than fifteen or sixteen.

"Why would these photos be separate from the ones my father had framed in his house?" Rose says. "There are more."

Herman and the girl are at least a couple of years older in the next photo. He's sporting a beard and she's dressed up in high heels and a long wool coat. There's snow on the ground, and they're in front of a two-story house. Their arms are around each other.

"The letters my cousin translated cover a number of years, too," Rose says. "Some, from Denmark, appear to be written to my dad while he was still in Germany, and others are letters from Germany to him in Denmark. It's all very confusing."

"Too confusing to examine here," I say. "Do you mind if I take this box home with me?"

"Of course not. But while we're here, let's at least look at some of the objects together."

"Don't get the wrong idea, Rose. I feel privileged that

you're sharing this with me, and I want to go over all of it with you. I'd like to get my bearings first, and try to sort this out chronologically. But you seem awfully nervous about it."

"Admittedly, these photos were taken long before I was born, and on another continent, probably," she says. "But I'm shocked that it shows a life my father never talked about. This girl seems close to him."

"Maybe just a romance he'd closed the door on many years ago," I say. "Not that surprising."

"That doesn't bother me as much as a couple of the letters he wrote from New York, about five years ago," she says. "He appears very much afraid."

She rustles through the box to find the originals, then looks for the yellow legal paper in English.

"I can't find what I want," she says. This woman is not in good shape. She tries to put her coffee cup on one of the other tables, but misses. Milt's around to pick up the spills almost immediately. Before he bends down with his roll of paper towels, he glances at the door.

"Watch it, Ruby. Your worst nightmare's here with some of the yentas."

"Yentas?" I can't help smiling at that one, even as I get a shreck in the pit of my stomach.

"Don't think I haven't learned something from twenty-odd years around you," he says, at the same time positioning himself directly in front of me and making a commotion as he cleans up the coffee.

I have just enough time to scoop up all the papers and put the box back into the big grocery bag Rose brought it in. Milt, as he always does when this particular yenta drops in, disappears into the kitchen.

"Ruby and Rose—I didn't know you two were such big buddies."

Essie Sue, who's with three of the more fashionable

Temple Rita members, drops her purse and her friends at an adjoining table and sweeps over to our humble hideaway in the corner.

"We're catching up," I say, literally covering my tracks with my feet. The large paper bag is under the table, where I'm using it as a footstool.

"You're very fortunate, Rose," Essie Sue says. "Ruby never has time for me."

"You look popular enough," I say, motioning to her girlfriends at the next table. They're busy whispering and filling each other in as to who Rose is, I'm sure, with all the gory details about Herman.

"Can you believe, Rose, that in a few months our little students will be Bar and Bat Mitzvahed?"

"Well, it's not until late May, Essie Sue," Rose says. "That seems a long time to me these days."

"Not long enough to do all the reception planning, dear. Especially since our catering is in such disarray."

That's tactful. I'm afraid the next thing out of her mouth will be disappointment that Essie Sue's personal caterer has died and caused all this inconvenience. Never mind that he was a beloved father and grandfather. I know the ceremony will be bittersweet for Rose, without her father there.

I can tell that she isn't used to the everyday sparring necessary to keep Essie Sue at bay—she hasn't opened her mouth. Before she begins making motions to leave—one of the more common reactions our friend evokes—I lean over and tell her quickly that I think we should stay for a bit.

Fortunately, Rose gets it. Essie Sue might be obnoxious, but she's also sharp, and I don't want to be caught making an exit with all the paraphernalia showing. With my luck, I'd get clumsy and drop the bag. We're stuck here for a few minutes at least.

"Are you eating, Ruby?"

I can't tell if this is her way of monitoring my diet in

public, something she's perfectly capable of doing, or if she wants to know whether we're coming or going.

"We've finished," I say. She drums winter-purple fingernails on the table.

"New manicure?" Rose finds her tongue.

"Just now got it. Effusive Eggplant—it's a new shade. Our group goes to the beauty shop together for manicures, and then out for coffee."

"Do you all have it?" I say.

"Effusive Eggplant? Well, as a matter of fact, yes. It's new."

As if that explains it, and I guess it does.

"All except Doreen," she remembers. "She's in mourning."

"That's not a mourning color? It's dark enough." Rose is getting into the spirit now.

"It calls attention to itself. I told her she needed Wuthering Whites for mourning. It's unpretentious."

We wince in unison. I don't know what Rose is thinking, but I'm thinking cremation.

"How do you know these things?" Rose asks.

"Some of us make the rules and the rest of us play by them," I say.

It's the one thing I've said all morning that Essie Sue agrees with.

"I simply have fashion sense, Ruby, and a commitment to propriety."

If Wuthering Whites represents propriety, I'll eat my unpolished nails, but I let it go. Eternal's arbiter of style won't be unseated in this life.

I raise an eyebrow in Rose's direction to let her know I'm preparing for a getaway, but then I get cold feet when I realize I have to subtly hoist the big paper bag that's under my seat. Milt's in view across the room and I put a lot of ESP into a long look at him. It works.

"How about showing Essie Sue our new salad display?" I say when he warily saunters to our table.

"It's glassed in," I say, "and refrigerated."

I can't imagine why Milt's giving me that incredulous glance—maybe it's because any salad display would no doubt be glassed in and refrigerated. But he comes through and leads her over, shaking his head at me as he goes. I have no doubt he'll collect from me in blood.

"Since it's a new display counter," Essie Sue asks him, "are you offering a discount on the salads? How about sesame noodle? My friends might want some, too, if you make it a special."

I leave him to fend for himself and grab the bag. Rose is ready to go and we're out the front door while Essie Sue's still haggling. At least one benefit of being part-owner is not having to waste time paying the bill.

chapter
35
....

I let Oy Vay run in the backyard so I can sit on the liv-
ing room floor and spread out the contents of the wooden
box. The piece is handmade, and looks like German crafts-
manship—faded in color but beautifully fitted. It smells
like cedar.

With the English translation as my guide, I try to sort the
materials chronologically. Rose's cousin has numbered the
pages in the yellow tablet to match numbers he's delicately
written on the original pages of the Yiddish and German.
Both languages were used—maybe at different times. I
look to see if everything's in the same handwriting, but it's
hard to tell—it's all so scrunched up and faint.

The collection is in two chunks—the items we gave the
cousin to translate, and which came from Herman's house,
and the pieces the cousin had forgotten about—those Herman gave him for safekeeping. I'm dealing in both cases
with four categories—photos, letters, postcards, and loose
diary or journal entries. Since I can see that not all the tex-
tual material is dated, I start with the photos and look for
the earliest.

I can tell right away that all the items Herman trusted to his cousin for safekeeping relate to the young blonde woman and maybe her family. When Rose and I were cleaning out Herman's house, we collected many photos from Herman's youth, but none of the images were of this young woman. So I'm assuming that the documents stored along with the photos of the girl all pertain to her as well.

Of course, I start with this chunk—the one with the mystery about it. I'm wondering why these letters and pictures had to be kept away from Herman's home.

I was looking at two of these photos in the bakery before Essie Sue interrupted us—one taken when Herman and the girlfriend were just kids, and the other when they might be late teens. There are also more photos taken in the snow— one in front of a large log cabin with black smoke coming out of two cylindrical tin smokestacks. Three men in work clothes, boots, and aprons are standing in front of the cabin—there's a family resemblance. No girl here, and no caption on the back.

Aha—I can give the girl a name now: Bertie. I suppose that's short for Berthe. It's written in German on the back of one of the photos where she's seated alone, and also on some of the others, which say *Herman* and Bertie. There's a papa and a mama, but they look more like Bertie than Herman. Papa might be one of the three men in front of the smokestack cottage—I'm not sure.

There are stamps on some of the letters, indicating two points of origin—Germany and Denmark—although I don't see any examples of the Danish language, only German and Yiddish.

I stack all the similar-looking photos together and then try to match them with the translations on the yellow pad. I'm assuming they were sent along with letters or saved with the journal entries.

Oy Vay's barking tells me it's getting late—she wants dinner. My front yard's bathed in twilight—the sun's setting in back of the Gordons' house across the street, and I feel I've barely begun sorting these papers. I have enough done, though, that I can put the piles in a safer place on the dining room table.

One of my neighbors calls to see if I want to take in a movie tonight with some of the girls, and I say no without ever thinking about it. I can tell this is going to be an all-nighter. Frankly, I couldn't be more content—I'm in my element. I'm definitely hooked.

If I thought the photos were fascinating, they're no match for the yellow pad. Rose's cousin has done a masterly job—that is, if I can assume the translation is accurate and not half made up to fill in the gaps. *Oy*—why do I have to be so cynical? Paul says it's the one character trait that's absolutely necessary for investigative work, but it also means I'm always second-guessing myself.

I'm hungry. I have some red cabbage in the house, and I quick-slice it into a big salad, adding some onion, green pepper, olive oil, rice vinegar, and a bit of feta on top. I set the whole thing on the dining room table away from the photos, and keep reading while I eat.

We knew Herman was the letter-writing type from his correspondence with the distributors, but apparently it was a lifelong trait. The translations on the yellow pad are selected letters from friends and relatives spanning almost sixty years. If these had been e-mails, they'd probably have been deleted and lost.

The earliest ones interest me most. They begin with Herman as a seventeen-year-old receiving shy declarations from what might surely be a first love, the girl named Bertie. From what I can piece together, Bertie and Herman had known each other in grade school, but were separated in their teens when her father moved the family to Denmark and joined relatives who owned a smokehouse. Bertie's two brothers were to learn how to cure fish, and perhaps to inherit the business from their uncle.

Bertie's family had been indifferent Lutherans in Germany, and Herman, of course, was Jewish. He makes no mention of any problem because of religion, and seems to have had a fondness for the family that was reciprocated.

The letters changed in tone a year later, when Herman moved to Denmark, south of Copenhagen. Letters from his mother indicate that his family was opposed at first, but gave in when they realized their son had already made enemies among his former schoolmates who had joined the Nazi party. Besides, Denmark was not so far away. Bertie's family were glad themselves to be away from the troubles in Germany, though they weren't personally affected. They offered to give Herman a job, and the two young people had planned to marry eventually.

There were few letters during the war years, but fragments of a personal journal survived:

> My travels to the German border have been too frequent this month. The woods beyond the railroad tracks are dense and dark—good for some purposes but producing many torn pant legs and shirts. I wash these myself. My mending is not skillful but I cannot ask Bertie. Her brother William asked about the gashes on my cheek from the sharp branches and I told him I had hurt myself on the metal hooks at work. As my boss, he insisted I should come to him right away next time I was clumsy.

Ed should see these materials—I wonder if Rose would let me show them to him. They round out the picture I had of Herman as someone who'd been a lifelong activist. He must have been young and strong enough to help Germans escape across the border into Denmark in the early years. And how alienating it must have been to have to hide this part of his life from the others.

I know Herman and Bertie didn't live together—it

wouldn't have been proper, for one thing, and there's a photo of them in front of a place captioned "my house"—with an upstairs window circled—his room in a board-inghouse, I'll bet. "Bertie's house" is featured in other photos—a larger one than the one in Germany, which seems to mean that the family profited from the move.

It's past midnight when I drag myself upstairs, having finished examining only a part of Rose's find. It's enough to convince me that Herman's life and death would make a fascinating article for Ed. And who knows what it might stir up?

As I drift into sleep, I realize, though, that I should have asked Rose to flag the letters written after Herman had left Europe for New York. The ones she found so alarming.

chapter
36

....

E-mail from: Ruby
To: Nan
Subject: *Our Current Obsession*

Remember you bet me that Paul Lundy wouldn't be interested in those old mementos of Herman's? You were right. And don't say I'm never a gracious loser. Too bad you didn't bet anything of value!

Rose had convinced me Paul would find something relevant in the box of stuff, and that I should show it to him before giving it to Ed. I guess you know Paul as well as I do after working with him so closely in the bagel bakers' case. Maybe better, since he seems to idealize you and think I'm in the way half the time.

Anyway, as you predicted, he told me that stories in old letters might be interesting, but were unlikely to provide much evidence.

Are you even up this early? If so, write me back before you go to work.

....

E-mail from: Nan
To: Ruby
Subject: *Obsession*

You're only a gracious loser when there's nothing at stake, Ruby. Next time, I'll wager with real money. I'm not surprised that Paul didn't see anything in old letters. It seems to me, though, that now's the time to show everything to Ed. And will Rose give permission? What about that letter you hadn't found—the one Herman wrote from NY?

I'm writing this from work—nobody's here yet and the office is quiet.

....

E-mail from: Ruby
To: Nan
Subject: *The Usual*

I had to give the box back to Rose before I finished going through everything—she wanted Paul to see it. On my advice, she did flag the letter for Paul to read, but she told me he wasn't impressed. I'm going over there tonight to read it, go through the box with her, and hopefully get her permission to let Ed examine it.

I have lots of questions for her. So will Ed, I'm sure, but he gets paid for it.

chapter
37

....

I run into Rose's husband, Ray, in the driveway—he's taking Jackie to her Bat Mitzvah class.

"How's your preparation going?" I ask Jackie. "Do you see Larry and Lester very often?"

"As little as possible," she says.

"Jackie—that's rude," Ray tells her, and then to me, "You know what it's like with seventh grade girls and the boys in their class."

Well, I do know what it's like with anyone normal and the twins, but I keep my mouth shut. Aside from a chuckle that I squelch and that Ray doesn't see.

"Rose tells me the boys are staying with you on the weekends," Ray says. "How's that working out?"

"Better than I thought it would when I got back from Alaska," I tell him. "You could say we have an agreement. Besides, they're only really sleeping at my house—Essie Sue's responsible for them the rest of the time."

"You mean you can get them to listen to you?" Jackie's incredulous. "I've tried to talk to them just to be nice and it's like throwing yourself into the middle of a full court press in a basketball game."

"We're working on it," I say.

What I don't say is that the little monsters and I have hammered out a truce based solely on self-interest—theirs. I discovered this practical streak in them right after they'd trashed my house and thoroughly intimidated Kevin. I gave them the choice of staying with Essie Sue on weekends or going home if they didn't shape up. When I saw that they really wanted to stay with me, I felt I had the upper hand, and told them so. Now even their beds are made in the morning when I check their room. I have no idea how long this hiatus will last. Obviously, it's not having much effect far beyond the confines of Watermelon Lane.

"Ruby? Coffee's ready." Rose waves me into the house.

"I've probably made Jackie late," I say.

"Don't worry about it. She likes you, which is more than I can say for most adults at this point in her life."

"She's a nice kid." And about three full years more mature than the twins. I can't believe they're the same age.

After I assure Rose I had dinner before coming over, she's content to serve me only dessert and coffee. The dessert turns out to be fruit and cheese, which is perfect, since I didn't have time for dinner, actually, and find no merit at all in having her dredge up a full meal for me. Dinner, if I'd had it, would have been tuna fish and cottage cheese, my usual when I'm in a hurry. I could write a book about the sea change in meal planning when your life goes from double to single.

I'm not able to wait a polite amount of time until we finish coffee.

"Can I please see the diary page about Herman's being frightened?" I say. "I'll be careful not to spill coffee on anything."

She hands me a three-page document—it's about five

years old. The first page is a newsletter of some kind, the second is a handwritten postcard, and the third is typed.

The newsletter's from Zabar's—some kind of house organ, I think, touting special Nova salmon cured in salt and sugar, then cold smoked with natural wood. It can be hand-sliced by one of the store's European experts—three men are mentioned, and Herman Guenther is one of them.

The item attached to the newsletter is a postcard of Times Square at night, dated, and postmarked from Bangor, Maine:

> *So Herman Guenther's in America. Please forward this to him.*

The postcard is unsigned with no return address.

The typewritten page is printed with the letters slanted upward as if the page had been inserted hastily and appears to be a journal entry:

> This frightens me. After all these years, and from one of us. As if my own guilt and sorrow weren't enough.
>
> How could someone in the publicity department put my name in a publication without mentioning it to me or getting my permission?

I look at the documents, and then at Rose.

"So what do you think?" she says.

"I'm trying to figure out what we know from these papers that we didn't know before about your father," I say. "He didn't like his name publicized, and someone has found out he's living in New York. Someone who frightens him."

"To learn this about a murdered man," Rose says, "isn't that something the police should be interested in?"

"It is five years old," I say. "I suppose Paul has the same

problem with it that he had with the prewar material. I mean, what can the police really do with it? They don't have the resources to chase down leads that old."

"So who does?"

I guess this is my opening.

"You know, Rose, I think this might be the time to get Ed Levinger involved. This is the point in an investigation where it's either gonna go somewhere or nowhere, and this one certainly doesn't seem to be moving. Maybe some publicity won't hurt."

"Just what my father didn't want," she says. "Not that it matters now."

"It is ironic, but I do feel that's the key to this. Whatever it was Herman wanted hidden needs to be exposed. And investigative reporters are experts at that."

"Sure," she says. "Ask him. But why would he be interested the second time around?"

"Because it's a much bigger story now."

I don't want to dwell on the fact that this is a murder, therefore opportune for prime time, so I change the subject. I've received her permission, and I don't want her changing her mind.

"I want to see the papers I wasn't able to read the other night," I say.

We pour over the yellow pad once more, reading all the translations. Herman refers several times to a life ahead with Bertie, and appears to be a part of the family already. Nothing's as provocative as the postcard, although I do find a souvenir worth noting. It's a bracelet.

"This has to be Bertie's," Rose says, "don't you think? She's the only woman he mentions."

"I guess it could belong to your mother," I say, "but it's unlikely, since this was in the box he gave to your cousin for safekeeping."

"He was certainly obsessed with Bertie," she says.

"Yeah, Rose, but if we've covered almost every item in this box, don't you find something odd, especially since he was so preoccupied with her?"

"Well, I can see in a way why he wanted to hide these things, can't you?" she says. "Maybe he didn't want my mother to be jealous."

"I'm still puzzled. We read lots about the romance in the early materials, but nothing in the later years. I can't understand why, in Herman's twenties and before he met your mother, we don't hear *more* about Bertie, not less. And what's bothering me isn't what appears in the box, but what doesn't."

chapter
38

·····················

I've promised the twins to watch one of their Bar
Mitzvah practices, although Valentine's Day seems rather
early to me. Today's some sort of teachers' day in Buda,
and the boys slept at my house last night before their nine
o'clock appointment at the Temple this morning. I offered
to drive them over, and I'm pulling into the Temple Rita
parking lot when Lester brings out something from his
book bag.

"Happy Valentine's Day," he says.

"It's not just from Lester, it's from me, too," Larry says.

I open the sealed baggie that's being thrust at me—it's a
gigantic red sugar cookie in the shape of a heart—except
that the bottom point of the heart has been bitten off. Apparently, they've forgotten about the bite until now.

"He did it," they say, each pointing at the other.

"We bought it ourselves in Buda," Larry says. "At the
7-Eleven, and I didn't take that bite."

"Hey, maybe Oy Vay ate some of it," Lester says.

"It doesn't matter, boys, I love it just the same."

"Take a bite," they say, and I do, passing it to them. In an instant, it's demolished, which is a shame since I wish I could keep it. Maybe my tough love policy is making a dent. I knew they wanted to stay with me, but hey, I'd want to stay with me, too, if the other choices were Essie Sue and Kevin. This is the first sweet gesture I've ever seen them make.

"We're supposed to go to the big room," they say.

"You mean the sanctuary? Where the Ark is?"

"Yeah, where our Bar Mitzvah will be."

We walk into the empty space and I must admit I'm having trouble picturing the ceremony to come.

Apparently I'm alone in that thought, because the next voice I hear couldn't be more confident.

"Let's don't waste any time, boys. I'm ready to give you your lesson."

I'm expecting Kevin, but I'm getting Essie Sue. No thank-you's for bringing the twins over, but that would be out of character.

"What lesson, Essie Sue? I thought they had a meeting with the rabbi."

"Nope, with me."

"She's teaching us to walk," Larry says.

"I recently learned, Ruby, that Rabbi Kapstein's instruction is entirely cerebral."

"That sounds about right, although I've never heard it put that way."

"Well, how are these young people going to appear before the whole congregation without some physical training? When they come down the aisle, I want them to walk in measured steps. I'm very good at this. Watch, boys, and I'll show you."

I interrupt the step-pause, step-pause routine.

"That's for weddings, Essie Sue. The Bar Mitzvah boys won't be marching down the aisle. That's not what they do."

"You're wrong as usual, Ruby. They walk the sacred scrolls around with the rabbi and they leave the sanctuary when the service is over. Come on, boys."

She pushes them down the aisle, but they balk.

"Ruby says we don't have to," Larry says.

"See the kind of influence you are, Ruby? I'm trying to teach them dignity, and you interfere."

"They'll be a laughingstock," I say.

Kevin sticks a hesitant head in the doorway, and for once, I'm glad to see him.

"Come in here, Rabbi, and straighten Ruby out." Essie Sue drags him into the room.

"I've got an appointment," he says.

"This is your appointment."

He looks at me, but I can't help. "Ruby, I tried to tell her that this isn't part of the service, but she wouldn't listen."

"Well, it should be," she says. "This is an important part of their training to be men, and it should be added to the curriculum."

"Before they've even learned their Torah portion?" I ask.

Larry and Lester have wisely taken advantage of the melee and vanished.

"It's your fault, Ruby."

"I wouldn't antagonize the person in charge of their sleeping arrangements if I were you," I say. "So are you telling me," I say to Kevin, "that they didn't have a meeting with you today, and I've wasted my time?"

"No, they had one with Essie Sue, not me. I told her not to do it."

"What are you here for then, Kevin?"

"I saw your car. I wanted to tell you that your boyfriend called trying to find you."

I'm trusting the twins to find their own way out of this—they're not exactly amateurs at eluding Essie Sue's orders.

Since I'm much more interested in talking to Ed, I get out fast. I head back to the car and use my cell phone, wondering why he called me at the Temple.

"Why didn't you call the cell?" I ask.

"Because you weren't picking up, and I didn't want to wait for you to answer your voice mail. I remembered you said the twins had to be at Temple this morning."

"Yeah, I dropped them off. I'm finished here, though."

"How about a Valentine's Day lunch?"

"You got my card in your mail this morning, right?"

"Guilty. And by the way, I did remember on my own—I just couldn't get the scheduling to work out for tonight. It happens that I'm in Austin for work—can I drive down to Eternal?"

"Ed, if you're already here, why can't you stay until to-morrow?"

"I have to get back home to San Antonio for a meeting this afternoon—it's a command performance."

"So when you said *lunch,* you really meant *only* lunch, yes?"

"Afraid so. Come on, Ruby. Don't give me a hard time."

"Sure. Where do you want to meet?"

"Why don't we have lunch on your deck? The weather's still nice. I'll stop and get some stuff—even the lemonade."

"This means you don't want to wait at a restaurant, not that you want the privacy of my deck. You only have an hour, I'll bet."

"About that. I'm really sorry."

"Okay, see you soon."

I'm beginning to think the twins' cookie was more spon-taneous. I know Ed got my card and figured he'd better do something fast. It's not the Valentine's Day shtick—I couldn't care less about that when other things are working out. My biggest gripe with him is that I know he comes to Austin on business a lot more than he tells me—this is only proof of all the times he *doesn't* stop. But I'm still at the place where seeing him is better than not seeing him. For now, anyway.

chapter
39

....

Austin is only twenty minutes away if you drive like
Ed does, so I barely have time to get home and clear the
breakfast dishes. By now, though, I've decided to do exactly what I've been telling everyone I'd do—talk to Ed
about the Guenther case. An hour's time over lunch is perfect—forget the Valentine's Day part. He wouldn't even be
bringing lunch if he had more romantic things in mind, so
I'll take him on his own terms.

He brings chicken salad sandwich plates from one of
The Hot Bagel's competitors, with large lemonades. And
two big cookies. Valentine cookies. Red ones. Yep.

It would be really nice of me not to bring up the fact that
Larry and Lester beat him to it, but in certain circumstances, I'm not that nice. He takes it well, which of course
I knew he would, not having too many deficiencies in the
self-esteem department.

"I guess you're wondering where that guy went who
danced to 'Stardust' with you on the cruise," he says.

It's insights like this, where he beats me at my own
game, that endear this man to me. But because he's pin-

pointed the problem doesn't mean I'm letting him get away with it. Or that I'm going to turn it into a beating-up session, either. My own self-esteem doesn't demand that.

"Good chicken salad," I say. "My favorite. . . . We've got about forty-five minutes left, Ed, if you need to stick to the one-hour lunch, and I really do have something important to go over with you about Herman's murder case."

I'm thinking he can even deduct the lunch, since this is definitely business. But I don't point this out—I have my standards.

He's clearly surprised that I don't pick up on the mea culpa, but he's game.

"Go for it," he says. "I really wish I had more time, but I'll be late if I wait any longer than that."

It takes all the remaining time to tell him about the Yiddish and German translations. I try to hit the highlights, and then if he's still interested, I'll have Rose give him the documents. I go over the prewar letter from Herman describing his trips to the German-Danish border, the Zabar's publicity that he hated so, and the postcard from Maine indicating someone he feared knew he was in New York. I remind him that Essie Sue had, unknown to Herman, also put his name and picture out over the Internet.

"Both tracks look promising to me," I say, "the old documents and the Alaska distributors' connection. The Alaska meeting would seem less promising except for what happened to us at the gold mine."

He's got that hungry look again, and it's not for chicken salad.

"What did Lundy say?" he asks.

I tell him that Paul felt hampered by the age of the translated material, but that he was following up Herman's grievances with the lox people.

"Whaddaya think?" I say.

"The murder drives it, of course," he says. "I've got to

admit Rose's documents make damn good background to that."

"Yeah, and what about the fact that Herman's girlfriend is never mentioned after the war? If she'd been killed, what's the big secret? And since she was a non-Jew living in Denmark, why *would* she be killed anyway? Was she helping him? It didn't sound so."

"I'd love to know if the family came over here after the war," Ed says.

"Which family?"

"Either the rest of Herman's family or Bertie's. Do we have the family names?"

"Oh, sure, there's plenty of that. All the early material contains names, places, descriptions, photos—*everything*."

"I've got a new assistant who's a whiz at researching on the Net. I'm gonna see what we can dig up."

"Does that mean you'll ask for the assignment?"

"One thing at a time. I can lay the foundation for a story on my own. And with the material Rose has, we know where to start. How about giving me her phone number?"

"I want to come with you when you talk to her."

We're more in sync than we've been all morning—I have to admit there's nothing more seductive to either one of us than the lure of a good trail to follow.

"Sure, you should go with me. She'll be more relaxed with you around. So am I."

Well, it's good to know I relax both Rose and Ed, even though I'm afraid Rose has no chance at all of getting the kind of kiss I just got from her interviewer.

chapter
40

· ·

E-mail from: Nan
To: Ruby
Subject: *Slow-Mo?*

Ruby, do you remember writing me at two in the morning yesterday and telling me nothing except that you just dreamed of Ed in slow motion? I'm thinking you might have been sleep-mailing. If you're awake now, I'd like more details. Geez.

· ·

E-mail from: Ruby
To: Nan
Subject: *Slow-Mo*

Didn't anyone ever tell you the *devil's in the details*?

· ·

E-mail from: Nan
To: Ruby
Subject: *Slow-Mo*

So is this dreaming simply out of pure frustration? From what I can see, you don't spend anywhere near enough time with this guy. What are you going to do about it? Somehow, writing your best friend in the middle of the night doesn't seem to be the right way to move this along. And don't change the subject, either.

••

E-mail from: Ruby
To: Nan
Subject: *Fast Work*

Maybe your e-mail set some kind of ESP going, down San Antonio way. If so, I know where you can get a lot of work on the psychic network. Right after your last message, I received one from Ed, saying: "Wanna go on a quick trip to NY with me?"

I wrote him back, wanting to know more, and received a cryptic reply:

"I need to chase down some folks we found on the Net, and I think I can scare up the money for both of us to go, if you're up for it. I'll call you tomorrow night."

I'm dying to know more, but I will not call him before I hear from him first.

Nan, this has to have something to do with the Herman business. We met with Rose last week, and she filled in a few details for Ed before giving him the materials to look over. I've been antsy ever since, wondering if he'll be more enthusiastic than Paul was. After all, this is a story for him, not a homicide case as it is for Paul. Herman confided in Ed way back, and I'm still betting Ed feels obligated on some level.

....

E-mail from: Nan
To: Ruby
Subject: *Wow*

I'm overcome by my own powers. Since it's my ESP that's bringing you this trip, I expect to be filled in completely as soon as you speak to Ed.

What do you suppose "quick trip" means? A long weekend?

You can also kill both birds by telling Essie Sue you'll put in a lox order for the Bar Mitzvah, since you didn't nail one down on the West Coast.

chapter
41
....

Ed phones tonight as he said he would, although he's a bit on the late side at 11 P.M. I'm reading in bed as always at this hour, with Oy Vay asleep at my feet. Since we often talk late at night, I'm not startled, though I have to admit I've been super-wired all evening, waiting for this call. As usual, Ed doesn't waste time getting to the point.

"Honey, my assistant here got online this week and tracked down some of the family names Rose gave me. She looked at East Coast directories, concentrating on Maine and New York. I also wanted to see if some of the names appeared on immigration lists from the immediate post–World War II years. We rechecked those with trade organizations having to do with the processing of fish. I've come up with one family owning a smokehouse in New Jersey. They sell lox to some of the finest delicatessens in Manhattan."

"Are they Herman's family or Bertie's?"

"They'd have to be Bertie's, but who knows after all these years? I can't think of a greater long shot, but it's so amazing to me to have come up with any match at all that

I'm really tempted to go up there. I can't believe I could approach them by letter or phone and get the kind of response I want. If this has anything to do with what was frightening Herman, a lot more delicacy's required, don't you think?"

"Absolutely. You know, I was telling Nan about your e-mail, and she had what I think is a stroke of genius. She said I could have a good excuse to go East by telling Essie Sue I was putting in a lox order for the Bar Mitzvah, since the Alaska connection fell through."

"Which is exactly why I wanted to see if you were up for going along. I wasn't thinking exactly along those lines, but I figured your being an owner of a deli would give us the very cover we need not to make a stir when we first meet these people. If we do get to meet them."

"Do you realize how wild it is to be able to match lists like this on the Internet? It's changed everything."

"Except old-fashioned footwork, which is the logical next step—no pun intended. I've talked to my editor, and I can make a case for this. I'm also covering something more prosaic for them while I'm up there, just to cover my ass on expenses."

"And you can scrounge up my airfare?"

"If we get a good price, I can do it, and the rest of your expenses can easily merge with mine. Unless you'll insist on your own room."

I can palpably feel what's coming across the phone lines.

"Um—I can make any sacrifice if I have to. And you?"

After hearing in exquisite detail the extent of Ed's willingness to sacrifice, I'm content to lie here after the phone call and contemplate our trip. Too bad it's only four days.

I'm also realizing that this is not such a total long shot. We would be foolish to rely simply upon Herman's journal in which he talked about being frightened because Zabar's published his name, or even the resulting postcard from someone who now knew he was in this country. But we have much more recent evidence of his fears. He was furious when he learned that Essie Sue had submitted a photo of him in the local paper last year while he was doing a catering job for the Temple. Not to mention what he never found out—that she'd also published a picture of him as a young man on the Internet.

Herman had something to hide, and I think we'd be remiss not to follow up on it. At the same time, though, I'm hoping Ed will take another look at the fish distributors Herman threatened. Maybe they threatened him, too, and we simply haven't found that piece of the puzzle.

I'm drifting off to what seems like five minutes of deep sleep when the phone rings again. I flail my arms until the receiver somehow ends up in my hand.

"Ruby? Are you up?"

"Huh?"

"Are you awake?"

"Probably not. It's the middle of the night."

"It is not. It's six in the morning. I've already had my coffee."

There's a maddeningly familiar tone to the voice on the line.

"Essie Sue?"

"Of course. I certainly don't have to identify myself after all these years you've known me."

That goes by me. "What's the matter?"

"There's nothing the matter, Ruby—don't be so pessimistic."

"I'm half-dead, Essie Sue. You'd better be bringing me to life for a good reason."

"You go to sleep too late for normal people—I'm always having to tell you that."

"Don't talk to me about normal people at this hour, okay? What are you calling for?"

"I have a wonderful idea for the boys' Bar Mitzvah. I'm going to ask Rose to join us in a joint celebration. The rabbi has already agreed to perform a double ceremony, just like they do in the big temples. And we can give the Oneg Shabbat reception together—it should cost Rose much less money. I'm doing it in Herman's memory."

That's it? I can barely rouse myself to answer, but I try. Otherwise, she'll call back—I know from bitter experience.

"They do double ceremonies in the big temples because they have too many members to accommodate people's schedules, Essie Sue. But are you offering to pay for Rose's share of the Oneg, too?"

"Should I?"

"First, you need to see if she wants to do a double ceremony, which I doubt."

I'm thinking of Jackie having to share with Larry and Lester, her favorites. "Then you need to be tactful about it, Essie Sue." Ha. "But I know for a fact she could use the financial help."

"I'll call her."

"No. Let me talk to her first. And certainly don't call her at this ungodly hour. I've got to go back to sleep now."

"Don't hang up. We have to talk about the catering if I'm paying for two ceremonies."

"I might have an angle on ordering something from New York, Essie Sue. You'll be happy about it. But now let me off the phone. Bye."

"Early to bed, early to rise, makes a person healthy, wealthy, and wise, Ruby."

She might be rich, but one out of three definitely isn't enough to convince me.

chapter
42

....

We're staying on the third floor of a brownstone on East Ninety-second Street, across from the Jewish Museum, a fabulous break for us since it's basically free. I guess I could have also called my husband Stu's relatives on the West Side, but since they've never quite gotten over his death and since I'm here with Ed, that didn't seem to be such a great idea. We were about to book a one- or two-star hotel to save money, when Ed heard unexpectedly that a colleague of his in New York was flying to Belgium on assignment for a week. They've done favors for each other over the years, and the guy was more than happy to let us stay at his place.

The apartment was designed around a huge bathroom, from what I can fathom. So many of these old brownstones were chopped to pieces, with apartments made from every room in the house. You can always walk into one and know immediately whether it was originally the kitchen, a guest bedroom, a master, or whatever, because those fixtures are central, with little rooms carved around them. I have to admit I've never seen one built around a bathroom. The space for the huge tub, sink, toilet, and cabinet is proportionally the biggest room in the place. Off one side of the ornate bathroom is a small living room, and off the other side is a curtained bedroom with a futon. The kitchen is minuscule.

We love it, especially since we don't have to live here more than a week. I, however, could get used to it in an instant if it meant having access to so much, but I'm sure I could never afford the location.

Though my relatives wouldn't think of living anywhere but the West Side, I happen to be very fond of this part of the Upper East Side. It's a friendly neighborhood and an easy walk east to several little family-owned restaurants on Second and Third Avenues. The 92nd Street Y is also really close, though I don't know if we'll have time to drop in on some of their neat authors' panels, assuming we could get in.

Ed's always loved New York, too, so we're both in a good mood—I hope it stays that way. We're home from dinner and another long walk down Fifth and back up Madison, and we bought a good Pinot Noir to share. This is our night to plot strategy, of which we have none—so we'll have to invent it.

"Okay," I say as I sip our pretty fair choice, "this is what I think we should do. Or maybe what I'm certain we shouldn't do. We shouldn't actually knock on the door, so to speak, until we've asked around and checked them out. I'm afraid we'll get thrown out."

"Not if you're thinking of ordering," Ed says, "then you'll be a customer and well treated. Of course, you're correct, I guess—if we took that route, you couldn't really ask any personal questions."

"Right. Let's don't limit ourselves until we see who they are in their neighborhood."

"Maybe we should go out there tomorrow," Ed says, "and drop in everywhere but the smokehouse."

"Not too close, though—definitely not the two establish-ments right next door to the place."

"I thought investigative reporters were crafty," he says. "We're known as slime in most quarters. Where did you take *your* lessons?"

"I'm a born snoop—it comes naturally to me."

"Then let's do it—we have the car, too."

Our apartment friend's also letting us use his Accord, parked in a nearby garage. Ed's not edgy about Manhattan traffic like I am, and he's familiar with the main arteries and tunnels to get us out of here.

After a very agreeable night touring vistas of a much more personal nature, we're zipping over to New Jersey to see the neighborhood around the smokehouse.

"They have a very complete site on the Web," Ed says.

"Why didn't you give it to me before we left? I'd have checked it out on my own."

"I forgot, and besides, this was planned so fast. The site has an order section, features of all their specialties, and a history page about the place being a family-owned business."

"Bertie's family name was Steuben. Is that what you traced?"

"There were Steubens and also some cousins who came over at about the same time. They might have gone into business together. Anyway, the history page says that the former owners of the smokehouse were people named Levin. I'm assuming they were Jews, since a lot of Jews had smokehouses in the old days. The Steubens bought the company from them."

While we're yakking, we're halfway to Jersey already, making such good time this morning that I'm wanting to stop somewhere for an early lunch. Ed's up for lunch, too, but wants to wait until we're in the right neighborhood, so I rein in my hunger.

With the help of the map, we close in on our prey and

before long we're cruising a commercial district dotted with low-slung buildings. One of them has a sign saying STEUBEN FAMILY SMOKEHOUSE—OLD WORLD FLAVORS. There are cars parked outside, but no people coming in or out. We note and pass it, driving four or five blocks before we see something that looks like a restaurant. It's an omelet place, and in my opinion, is precisely the right thing for late morning.

"How about it?" Ed says.

"I doubt if we'll find much better," I say. "Let's go for it."

We pull up into the barely filled parking lot, and I can tell we'll miss the midday rush.

"Yeah?" The waitress looks like she's been on her feet too long—several years too long. The *yeah* isn't even unpleasant, it's just an abbreviated way of saying what in Texas would be "whadda y'all want today?" I find that some of what visitors define as rude in the New York area is really just a local shorthand that works well for the natives but sounds lousy when you try to analyze it.

"What's good?" I say. "We're not from around here."

"You like salami? Try the salami and onion omelet. It's good."

"Is lox and onion good, too?" Ed says.

"Yeah. It's very good."

We order two, along with rye toast and coffee.

"Clever," I say. "Now we can bring up the subject of fish."

"Nice of you to notice," he says. "I thought it might be a good idea."

The food comes fast, along with an unordered side of coleslaw and pickles. The eggs are hot and absolutely delicious.

"What's in the rye bread here," Ed says, "that's so much better than anything we can get?"

"Ha—the question of the century. Milt and I have tried more rye breads than your laptop has keys, and we still can't get anything that compares. There's a certain chewiness in this bread that has flavor attached to it and that doesn't travel—that's all I can tell you. Maybe it's the ovens and maybe it's the water. A mystery."

"I tried in Miami once," he says. "If not there, where? And of course they swore their rye could compare with New York's any day. I had news for them. It didn't."

"Good lox," we say when the waitress brings us our check.

"We're in the business," I say. "Do you know where this comes from?"

"The manager would," she says. "He's at the cash register."

We leave a tip at the table and approach a skinny guy in a well-worn black Deadhead T-shirt. I don't think he eats here—either that or his metabolism's in overdrive. I've probably gained more from this meal than he weighs on a good day. Fortunately, though, there's no line ahead of us and he doesn't appear rushed.

"We thought the lox was extra special," I say. "Where do you get it?"

"Where do I get it? By refrigerated truck, twice a week. It flies out the door."

"We're in the deli business," Ed says.

The guy doesn't seem all that impressed. He nods. "But not from Jersey, right?"

"Definitely not from Jersey." I smile, then the guy makes a face that I realize *is* his version of a smile.

"Glad to hear you're not competition," he says. "A couple of those threatened to move in lately."

I'm tempted to assure him we won't make an offer he can't refuse, but I can tell Ed's already anticipating and discouraging any wisecracks on my part. He knows me too well. Now that I think of it, after my previous experience with the West Coast fish distributors, I shouldn't need any warnings.

"There's a few places," he says. "But we get ours from Steuben's down a few blocks. We're so close they drop it by for free as long as we use our dolly and haul it off the truck."

"They sound okay," Ed says.

"Yeah, no gripes. I liked the old owners better, though. They retired and the Steubens wanted to put on a delivery charge, but we got it straight."

I guess we're both thinking at the same time that it's not such a great idea to ask more questions. This way, he'll forget about it. We give a casual thanks and leave.

"I'm glad you didn't follow that up," Ed says when we're back in the car. "I find it's better to use one tip to get another."

"You're right. Well, do we walk or ride?" I say.

"You're asking questions instead of making statements, Ruby. To what do I owe the pleasure of all this deference to me? I'm not used to it." He leans down and plants a kiss on my lips. It's loxy.

"Oh, I figure it's your story, and you did invite me along—not the other way around. That's all."

"Well, I hope you don't make a habit of it—I might not know who you are. But in answer to your question, I honestly don't think anybody walks around here. It's not that kind of neighborhood."

"I can't decide which way we'd be more conspicuous, driving back and forth or walking. I guess we could end up doing both, so you're probably right. Let's scout out the area again, and then maybe we could look as if we're walking back to our car from somewhere."

We don't have to decide at all. We hear the wail of sirens and follow them. A small crowd has begun to swirl, only a block from the Steuben Family Smokehouse. Two cops are busting a couple of punks who look to be in their early twenties.

"Perfect," Ed says. "There's nothing better than being able to work a crowd. Especially when we have an excuse for doing it—we can be onlookers just like everybody else here."

chapter
43

....

"They tried to rob the bodega," an old man tells us. *"I* was here before the cops even came."

"Did anyone get hurt?" I ask.

"No, thank God." That's from the woman standing beside him. "Luckily, a man was coming out just as these thieves came in. He thought they were looking for trouble and called the police just in case. He told them there was a robbery about to be in progress."

"I'm surprised they came so fast for something about to be," the man says. "They must've been in the neighborhood."

"Do you live on the block?" Ed asks him.

"Above that print shop. It's not a residential neighborhood anymore, but people still live here."

I guess I understand that.

"I've lived here for fifty years, and not always above a shop, either," the woman says.

"That Steuben Family Smokehouse on the next block—" I say, "someone told me they were old-timers, too."

"These people are not old-timers. The previous owners were—they'd been here even before we moved in. You Jewish?"

We nod yes.

"Well, the Steubens aren't," she says. "They bought it from some Jewish owners after they went into business with them, and couldn't get along."

"They didn't like Jews?" I ask.

"No, they were good friends for a while, but the children argued. You know."

"We know," I say. "We're in the deli business."

This, apropos of nothing, but the old couple nod anyway. Hopefully, it makes us sound more familial.

"They sell to a lot of delis," the woman says.

The small knot of people in front of the store is drifting away as we speak—especially after the police leave with the bad guys. Ed and I make an unspoken decision to stick with what we have—the rest of the crowd seems much younger than these two, and probably wouldn't be as talkative anyway.

"There were two brothers married to two sisters—they came over to this country after the war," the man says. "The sisters died and the men are in their eighties now. *Schtarkers.*"

"That's big, strong oxes," she translates for us in the younger generation. "They make them like that in the cold country where they came from. Iceland, I think. You should have seen them hauling those heavy slabs of fish. Like feathers to them."

Denmark, not Iceland, I'm thinking. "They're not going to retire in Florida or someplace?" I ask.

They both shrug. "You think they could afford that?" she says to him.

"Sure they could. But I would have heard on the street. No, they're still running the business. They'll never retire,"

Then he stands right next to Ed. "One of 'em is supposed to be a little bit *meshugge*. From my observation, he's just opinionated. The other indulges him."

"We're getting ready to go over and place an order," I tell her. "Anyone special we should ask for?"

"They have a receptionist. She's nicer than the owners—they don't give you the time of day."

We thank our new pals and move on.

"What do you think?" I ask Ed. "Do we stroll over to the next block and ask more questions?"

"Now that we've got some background, I'm worried about asking questions of someone who might be a friend of theirs. Let's go for it and park in their lot like customers. Our walking around will look weird if someone notices."

"We *were* thinking of coming back another day to do this," I say.

"Do you think that's necessary?"

"Frankly, no. We probably know as much as we're going to know."

We drive around the next block and pass the smokehouse again. There's a vacant lot in back with several cars parked. We pull into an open slot.

We avoid the more convenient back door and walk around to the front, since the receptionist is our interviewee of choice. At least for now.

We walk into a wood-paneled reception room with photos and posters on the walls. Déjà vu from the plant I saw in Kodiak, although this one in the smokehouse is more finely turned out. No one's at the desk, which gives us an opportunity to look around. The posters are copies of old catalogs, and the photos are black-and-whites featuring rather formal-looking men wearing overcoats and hats, and holding up what I'm assuming is smoked fish.

We don't get a chance to examine the pictures closely, because a girl balancing a coffee mug and some cookies in a napkin walks in from a door behind the counter. She's wearing a tight pink sweater and jeans so small they could fit a Toddler Two with no room to spare for the diapers.

"Hi," I say at the same time she does.

"I'm Ruby Rothman," I say. "I own The Hot Bagel bakery and deli, and I've come to ask about your finest Nova. I understand you supply some of the best establishments." I almost say I'm from Texas, but I don't want to give away everything at once before we meet the owners.

"Have you used our catalog?" she says. "People from out of town usually order by mail."

"We're ordering for a very particular customer," I say. "We were going to be in the area and she asked that we come ourselves and inquire about your specialty items. Maybe something rare and not featured for the general public."

Ed gives me a respectful look—it *was* a good improvisation. I think.

"It looks as if you've been in business a long time," Ed says as he points to the old photos. I'm figuring he's steering the conversation toward something we'd best not ask the owners at this point.

"We've been in business for almost sixty years," she says. "Our business used to be on the West Coast. We moved here a few years ago. But that's all in our catalog."

The phone rings and our receptionist excuses herself. It must be a boyfriend, because a big smile lights up her face and she snuggles the earpiece into her neck while she talks. I'm thinking this might take a while.

"You know," I whisper to Ed, "there were some things we were going to work out tonight back at the apartment. It just occurred to me why we said we should do this on two separate days. We don't have a plan. What if the owners come in? We don't even know if they're here. Do we say we're from Texas or not?"

"I guess I did jump the gun," Ed says. "But now that

we're here, I don't think we'd have much of an excuse to come back, do you?"

"Unfortunately, no. So think fast, darlin'."

"Let's stay awhile. Maybe she'll take us to look around. And if we meet the brothers, we'll feel them out and play it by ear."

It turns out we don't have any wiggle room at all, because the front door opens and a bent-over old man sprouting an uncooperative whitish-gray beard comes in. The beard's growing in crooked, and he's fiddling with it as if to force the growth back in the right direction.

"Mr. Sam," the receptionist says, slamming the phone back onto its base. I'm glad the ear on the other end isn't mine. "I was . . ."

"She was just showing us around," I say. "We're customers."

She looks at me gratefully. It's not hard to see that she's scared witless of her boss, who looks rather benign to me, but then I don't work for him.

"And the phone rang," she says, apparently still not sure she's safe. "It was a wrong number."

"A customer?" he says, extending his hand across me to Ed, who seems amused by the gesture. I'm not similarly amused, a fact Ed knows only too well.

"You must be in our database, then."

"No," I say, determined not to be cut off, despite my plans to be charming and keep him off his guard. "We're prospective customers."

"We heard you were the best," Ed says. "That you supply some of the big Manhattan stores."

"We are," Mr. Sam says, seemingly taking us at our word. "My brother and I own the business, and you're right—we have a good clientele. And you are—?"

I look at Ed briefly, and plunge in. "I'm a deli owner. We have a very special request from a valued customer—one of our mainstays, you understand, to use your products for her relatives' Bar Mitzvah celebration."

"Our smaller orders are handled by mail," he says. "I'm sure we can accommodate you from our catalog." Mr. Sam speaks with a German accent, but it's slight.

Ed moves a bit closer to him. "She wants bragging rights," he says. "Surely you're familiar with that. When she knew we would be in town for other business, she insisted we come here personally."

"Sam?" a booming voice from the back of the reception area yells out. Sam opens the door to the back area and gestures toward us.

"These are out-of-town customers," he says, and disappears into the back. He leaves the door open, so I'm assuming he's coming back.

"Who's that?" I ask the receptionist.

"The other one," she says, "Mr. Gustav. He's Mr. Sam's brother."

"Who runs the place?" Ed asks.

"Oh, Mr. Gustav does. He calls and we jump." I can see we're benefiting from not giving away her boyfriend's phone call, so I try for more.

Pretty good for a quick two minutes, but it's over when Mr. Gustav comes in, followed by Mr. Sam. Now this is a *beard*—all white, and it knows where it's growing, full all over with no hairs daring to be out of place. It doesn't match the hair on his head, though, which is obviously dyed a coal black.

I glance over at Ed, fully expecting to be thrown out of here any moment, but I'm wrong.

"This is my brother Gustav," Sam says.

Mr. Gustav gives Ed a beefy hand, also ignoring me. There are Orthodox Jews who won't shake hands with a woman, but these guys aren't even Jewish, so I have to conclude this omission is not for religious reasons.

"So you heard about our place," he says to Ed.

"We both did," Ed says with that look of his that tells me he can't wait to hear me explode when we get out of here.

"What can we do for you?" Mr. Gustav says.

To my surprise, Ed tells him he's a reporter. So far, neither of us have mentioned the Texas connection, and the conversation's so rapid-fire that Mr. Gustav doesn't ask. He does, though, seem very much interested in the publicity.

"We have had many articles and news stories about our facility," he tells Ed.

"I'd like to record the interview," Ed says.

I guess the neighbor who said the Steubens wouldn't give you the time of day was wrong—Mr. Gustav is apparently willing to make an exception for the press. He doesn't, however, agree to have his words recorded. Ed doesn't push because I'm sure he's not going to take the chance of getting thrown out of here. I'm wishing now that we had coordinated our approach, but since we haven't, I'm going to plunge in.

"These photos on the wall are fascinating," I say. "You must have been in business for a long time."

"For more than fifty years," he says, "but only five years in the East. My son married a New York girl and they had a grandchild for us. She wouldn't move out of New York, so we relocated."

"He makes it sound like nothing," Mr. Sam volunteers. "But what a tumult deciding to do it. I was ready to retire, but then we heard about this place and my brother thought we should try it. For the grandchild."

Oy, I can imagine how much say Mr. Sam must have had in all this.

Ed points to the photos again. "This looks like a smokehouse you're all standing in front of," he says. "Was it in Europe? And is this your family?"

"In Denmark, during the war. This is me," Mr. Gustav

points, "and this is my wife. That's Sam and his wife beside us."

"And this?" Ed asks.

"Our sister," Mr. Sam says, "she was killed in the war."

"Was it a bombing?" I say.

Mr. Gustav gives his brother a look I wouldn't want to wish on even my worst relatives. "She was killed as a *result* of the war," he says. "We don't talk about it."

"Might as well have been *in* the war," Mr. Sam says. "It killed her."

"We don't talk about it," Mr. Gustav repeats.

"Is this another brother her hand is reaching for?" Ed asks. He's looked at the photo more carefully than I have, and sure enough, someone on the end has been cut from the photo. You can see part of a shoe next to the sister's foot, but no corresponding figure.

Mr. Sam looks quickly at his brother, as if to stave off an eruption, but none comes. Instead, Mr. Gustav turns his back to the photos on the wall.

"Would you like a tour of the facilities?" he says. He points a huge hand toward the back of the office. It's a hand toughened and dark—I guess it's smacked around a lot of smoked fish. Hopefully, nothing else.

My first clue that this gesture is out of the ordinary is the receptionist's face—she jerks her head around as if she heard wrong. Then she looks at Mr. Sam, who shrugs, then looks at Mr. Gustav to make sure the shrug didn't show. It didn't. Mr. Gustav isn't paying attention to anything but us.

He puts his big arms around our backs, not touching but just guiding us through the back door of the reception room. But he's one of those men who doesn't need to touch—he rules by force field.

"Are you sure you have time for this?" Ed says. I'm thinking that he's taking a real chance here that Mr. Gustav will cancel our tour, but I know Ed well enough to see that he's testing just how much Mr. Gustav wants us to accompany him.

He needn't have bothered. We're herded through a doorway that leads outside into a courtyard. On one side is a large building, and on the other is a log cabin sitting on fake green grass.

"This is a working replica of a smokehouse," Mr. Gustav says. "It's like the one we had in Europe. This smokehouse was originally in Brooklyn, where a lot of people think the best lox and Nova come from."

"And our plant is over here," Mr. Sam says. "All modern. Nothing was for sale in Brooklyn when we wanted to come back from the West Coast, so we landed here in New Jersey."

"That's where you process the lox?" I ask.

"Among other things," Mr. Gustav says. "Lox is what they first sold from this old smokehouse—from Alaska. *Lox* comes from the German *lachs,* meaning salmon. It used to come barrel-packed in brine, so they had to soak off a lot of the salt. They sliced it thicker in those days, too.

"The big seller today is Nova," he says. "It costs more. We rub it with salt and brown sugar, and then cure it mildly for three or four days depending on where it comes from, and smoke it over a hardwood fire. For some salmon, we use wet brine before smoking, too."

"So what was it like in the old days?" I ask.

Mr. Gustav ignores me, and looks at Ed.

"Would you like to see our modern packing assembly?"

"I think we'd like to see the old-fashioned smokehouse now. It makes good copy."

Aha—I knew we were still in sync. In that atmosphere, we might still be able to get something out of him about the family, although we both know I need to shut up and let Ed ask the questions here in macho city.

I can sense Ed's mind riffling through the possibilities. On the one hand, as long as we're just visitors, I don't think this big, gruff old man is going to let much loose. But if we say too much, we could get kicked out. I give Ed a sympathetic look to let him know it's all right with me if he takes some risks. And I have no doubt that we understand each other.

Mr. Gustav stoops as he leads us through the narrow doorway of the replica—*narrow* being the operative word as he squeezes by. Either they made this structure slightly doll-sized or Mr. Gustav would have never fit into the old one—I'm not sure which. Ed follows, then me, then Mr. Sam.

"Are there lights in here?" I say, feeling claustrophobic already.

"They used lamps or natural light in the smokehouse," Mr. Sam answers. "We use electric lights now, but they're dim. You'll get used to it."

I doubt it—there's smoke curling from two pits at the end of the room, and I have no idea where it's escaping to. On second thought, I tell myself it's not all supposed to escape. It's a smokehouse, dummy.

There are a few paltry pieces of fish hanging over the pits just for show, but overall, the place *is* the pits.

Mr. Gustav starts in on a lecture about Atlantic and Pacific salmon, and how today they use more Pacific but that certain customers only want Atlantic.

"Did your family work together in the old smoke-house?" Ed says.

Our lecturer hasn't asked for questions, and replies that Atlantic salmon is usually more expensive wholesale, but that you can ruin it in the curing process if you don't know what you're doing.

I can't see Ed well in the gloaming here, but the outline of his jaw tells me he's about to venture into more precarious territory.

"We don't have anything like this in Texas," he says.

Mr. Sam jumps forward so fast he steps on my foot in the dark. "You're from Texas?"

"I'm from San Antonio," Ed says, "and Ms. Rothman's from the Austin area, where she owns a deli and bakery."

"Sam, these people seem uncomfortable. Wait for us in the office so it's not so crowded. And look at the files—maybe they've ordered from us before."

"No, we haven't," we both say at once, but by now, Mr. Sam's out the door, and with him goes our best chance to get some less controlled answers.

"So, tell me, Texans," Mr. Gustav says, putting a hand on each of us as we stand together in the middle of the room, "what do you need from us—a feature story, an order, or both?"

I'm holding my breath for two reasons. I'm feeling choked from this smoke, and I'm wondering what Ed's going to say next.

"I'll be frank with you—" he starts.

"That would be nice." Mr. Gustav is not playing the gracious host.

"We're here for an order because of your reputation, but also because of your name. A man who's the subject of an article I'm writing once worked for a Steuben family who owned a smokehouse in Denmark. Could that be you?"

"It's possible. His name?"

"Herman Guenther."

chapter
44

·······················

If Mr. Gustav is searching his memory bank, it cer-
tainly doesn't take long.

"I haven't made Mr. Guenther's acquaintance," he says.

"Perhaps one of the many workmen you've employed
through the years?" Ed's making a rational case against
such a rapid-fire answer, but Mr. Gustav remains unmoved.
If he were in a courtroom he might say "asked and answered," but to us he merely remains stone-faced.

I'm wondering what's going to come next, when the
door creaks open and Mr. Sam tentatively sticks his head in.

"I told you—" Mr. Gustav starts to wave him out again
when I get an inspiration, but it's going to take perfect timing to execute.

I take Mr. Sam's arm and bring him in, closing the door
behind him so he doesn't dart out, and turning my back to
Mr. Gustav.

"Mr. Sam, do you remember a Herman Guenther from
the old days?"

"Herman? How would you possibly know Herman

Guenther?" Then he claps his hand to his forehead. "Ach, *Gottenyu.* Texas."

Ed and I make quick eye contact, but that's all we can muster. In his own example of perfect timing, Mr. Gustav bolts from the smokehouse, pulls Mr. Sam along with him, and kicks the door shut.

I'm suddenly dizzy standing in the middle of the room, but Ed's arms are around me before I start to sway. He holds me up straight and I try to take a deep breath, but that's a mistake in this particular atmosphere.

"Holy smoke," he says.

My unexpected laugh makes me exhale instead of inhale, which is a blessing under the circumstances.

"Cut it out," I say.

"I guess it's a given that the door's not going to open," Ed says, "but we need to at least give it a try."

We go to the door and push together. It doesn't open.

"Don't panic," Ed says. "Let's think about what just happened."

"Huh? I say we start looking for windows."

"The place doesn't have any windows. You're still swaying. I think you should sit down."

I can't argue. As much as I hate to touch this smoky wooden floor, I plunk straight down, pulling Ed's hand so that he follows me.

"We need a time-out," he says.

"Okay, we're having it. If you're still asking what happened, I'd say that Mr. Gustav wants to get rid of us."

"I'm not ready to believe that yet. He's discovered we have some tie to Herman and that shocked him. I'm figuring he needs time to decide what to do about us. It makes no sense to kill two people who've visited his plant and may have told God knows how many people about it."

I take as deep a breath as I can take in this firetrap. "So what are we supposed to think about him?"

"Let's go with what we know. Herman obviously injured them in some way that's connected to their sister, Bertie. Maybe they even threatened him, and that's why he didn't want to be exposed in Essie Sue's article. That doesn't mean they killed him—he had other enemies, too."

"Uh-huh. And the way we prove he's not a killer is to see whether he kills us, right?"

"That's one way of looking at it. But killer or not, unless he's deranged, I don't believe he'll want to murder us right here on his property. My guess is he'll be back with some excuse."

"Yeah, but my little ploy with Mr. Sam made it perfectly clear that they not only knew Herman, but knew he was in Texas. And now they know that we know."

"So what? What can we really do to them because of that? We don't even know the whole story of their connection."

"And probably never will, now. I know one thing—I want out of here." I start pounding on the door.

"Keep it up," Ed says. "Maybe it'll make them nervous. And it'll give me time to look around for another way out."

I pick up a stick of wood to make the banging easier, and keep an eye on Ed, who's pushing and prodding on the side of the room where the fire pits are.

"Nothing," he says. "There's only one way out, apparently. I can't even find a water tap so I can put out the coals."

Before we can do anything else, the lights go out.

"Damn. They've cut the electricity," I yell.

"It's still daylight," he says. "There's a table here that I'm going to use as a battering ram on the wall. If this is a working replica, I doubt that they made it all that secure."

He lifts the table and throws it against the wall, which actually wobbles from the force.

"This is thin stuff," he says. "I'm on the right track."

It doesn't take too many wobbles before the front door opens.

"I can't believe you were right," I say.

"Thanks."

Sure enough, Mr. Sam and Mr. Gustav are standing in the doorway.

"The door stuck," Mr. Gustav says. "We hope you're all right."

We both rush out of the model smokehouse into the fresh air and sunlight, looking and smelling like prime specimens of cured Nova. Ed puts his arm around me.

We don't stay for explanations, but head for the front reception and office area and the exit.

"Sit down and have some water," Mr. Gustav says, all charm now. "You must be shaky from the accident."

"Some accident," I say.

To my surprise, Ed sits down, so I do, too. I guess it makes sense, now that the receptionist is a witness.

"I'd like some answers," he says.

Mr. Gustav is prepared. Even Mr. Sam looks calm now, so I'm sure we're about to get stonewalled.

"What would you like to know?" he says.

"For starters, why did you lock us in as soon as you realized we were from Herman Guenther's hometown?"

"My dear man, we didn't lock you in—it was an accident. And I told you I was unfamiliar with anyone by the name of Herman Guenther."

"But your brother wasn't," I say.

"What do you mean?" Mr. Sam says. "I don't know any such person either."

"Despite what we both heard you say?"

Mr. Gustav doesn't wait for Mr. Sam to answer me. "I don't know what you think you heard, but we don't know this individual. Right, Sam?"

Mr. Sam nods emphatically. "Absolutely right." I've never seen a man look more frightened in my life—if the look in Mr. Sam's eyes is any indication of what we're dealing with, we're lucky to be leaving on our feet. I'm unsinged, but definitely unhinged.

I want to bring up the so-called old days one more time, so I glance up at the wall. There's a white space where the photo of Bertie and her brothers used to be. Ed looks up, too.

We both stand at the same time, each convinced, I'm sure, that the denial has been neatly coordinated.

I walk out first, and Ed follows, with Mr. Gustav at the front door watching us leave.

"I'll make sure they get to their car," Mr. Sam says.

"We're parked out back," I say, taking his arm and making sure he goes out with us.

"It'll make a very interesting story for my newspaper," Ed says over his shoulder. Not much of a threat, but it's all we've got.

"Don't write that article," Mr. Sam tells Ed in a barely audible voice as he escorts us to the car. "You don't want to push my brother, believe me."

"Why? What's he capable of?" I say.

Mr. Sam looks back at Mr. Gustav standing at the back door and gives him an efficient wave, as if we're being sent off with dispatch.

He opens the car door for me.

"More," he says.

I look at Ed and we pull off, filling our borrowed car with the smudge of charcoal and the rancid stench of smoke. But we're out of there.

"I hope I don't look as creepy as you do," I tell him.

"You don't look as bad as you smell," he says.

"I'll bet this odor takes six months to disappear."

"If we're lucky. That was quick of you to bring Mr. Sam outside with us."

"What do you think he meant by 'more'?" I say. "What more could his brother do to us?"

"Let's rephrase the question," he says. "What has he done already?"

"I don't know, but I was suffocating in there."

"I know, honey," he says, taking my blackened hand and kissing it.

"So do you think it was worth it?"

"Oh, yeah," he says. "Absolutely."

chapter
45

· · · · · · · · · · · · · · · · · · · ·

E-mail from: Ruby
To: Nan
Subject: *Smoking Can Be Hazardous to Your Health*

More updates on the fallout from that fateful trip with Ed.
My cough is better today, but you'd swear my hair just
came off the barbecue grill. I've shampooed it a zillion
times and the smoke still lingers.

In answer to your last e-mail—no, Ed isn't going to
write an article. Not yet, that is. He's waiting until the police have more evidence in Herman's murder, and then
he's hoping to tie it all together. Meanwhile, he's doing
more research on the Brothers Grim and their processing
plant. And Rose is searching Herman's house one more
time to see if she overlooked anything.

What's up with you?

· ·

E-mail from: Nan
To: Ruby
Subject: *You Sound Encouraged*

I'm at work and hassled, but wanted to connect. Nothing's up with me—my social life is a cipher. On the work front, though, a good friend of mine from law school has asked me to consider a partnership. He's exactly the kind of person I'd like to work with, and we got along famously as students, but I know that's not the same as a professional setting. The good part is that he's got some seed money to put into this, which is something I certainly don't have at the moment. Whaddaya think?

You're sounding more upbeat about all the double-checking on the Herman research. Maybe it's simply being on your own home ground after that yucky experience. You did have fun with Ed during the first part of the trip, though—didn't you?

....

E-mail from: Ruby
To: Nan
Subject: Au Contraire

Yes, I had fun with Ed in New York, but in answer to your other observation, no, I'm discouraged, if anything. We sat down with Paul Lundy the other day when Ed drove up to Eternal, and gave him a full report on the New Jersey fiasco. He thought it was pure panic that the Steubens ran out of the smokehouse and closed the door, and that it certainly proves nothing specifically. He said it's possible they were the ones who threatened Herman when they discovered he lived in New York, and they were taken by surprise when we told them we had found a connection between them. Leaving us in the smokehouse for a few minutes gave them a chance to get together on a denial.

But we don't know why they were down on Herman, and we have more gaps than connections.

Paul also feels that there's a greater chance that the distributors Hermàn was warring with had someone kill him. It was a clean job, no fingerprints on the slicing blade or on anything in the kitchen, and could well have been a hit. Whatever it was, the police seem, in my opinion, to be writing it off. Well, not writing it off exactly, but thinking the case is getting very cold.

As for your partnership invitation, I've always felt that you'd be happy on your own, and working with someone compatible could be perfect. Let me know more of the details.

Meanwhile, it's show time here. The Levee twins are about to become men, you'll excuse the expression. Their combined Bar/Bat Mitzvah with Rose's daughter Jackie is imminent, and as usual, Essie Sue is driving everyone insane, with me number one on her list.

chapter
46

....

"*The husky department of the Big and Little shop* came through for me, Ruby," Essie Sue tells me as we go over her table diagram in the Temple social hall for the last time. "It took three long-distance calls to the store's Detroit management, but we overcame the torpid salespeople in Austin and ended up with three choices for the boys."

"You mean they sent you stuff direct from the headquarters?"

"No, they found the outfits in one of their California stores after the Austin manager resigned and we were left suitless."

"I don't even want to know the *skinny* on that one, if you'll pardon the expression," I say. "So, after only one resignation over this, you chose exactly what?"

"Black. With white shirts and charcoal gray neckties. Very formal. They also had blazers and tweed sport coats, but I wanted something representing the utmost seriousness and good taste."

I'm picturing little G-men or their opposite numbers in the Mafia. Which might fit, come to think of it.

"Blazers sound more appropriate for thirteen-year-old kids," I say. "What did the boys think?"

"After I saw them looking at shiny royal blue sweat suits, I didn't ask them for their opinion," she says. "I don't remember asking for yours, either, Ruby."

"Ah, yes, but you got it, anyway—your burden to bear as Eternal's arbiter of good taste. I can see your choice working for a funeral, though."

"You're never very helpful when it comes to taste, but I'll ignore that for now. I've got other worries. Like the lox presentation—Milt will never give me the beautiful platters Herman produced."

"Milt will do fine." I haven't told her why we ordered her lunch specialties from Los Angeles instead of the other coast—merely that the New Jersey people were too difficult to deal with. When she offered to negotiate with them herself, I said I'd heard rumors about the quality and value. Value's usually what ends up getting to her—she'd been squeezing poor Herman for every penny.

"Rose told me while you were away that she wanted to do some baking," Essie Sue says, "but I don't think she's very good—I felt safer ordering from professionals."

"Yeah, I heard," I say. I told Rose to bake what she wanted anyway—it's obvious to everyone but Essie Sue that people are going to be attracted to homemade goodies.

I'm losing interest fast. I said I'd help because I wanted to make sure Rose and Jackie weren't left out in Essie Sue's zeal to perform a good deed by shouldering most of the cost of the reception. Plus, I'm obligated to pitch in as a partner in The Hot Bagel, if only to support Milt, who's grudgingly doing most of the catering.

"Where's Kevin?" I ask. "I'd love to watch the twins practice for the big day Saturday. How're their speeches coming along?"

"You can't watch—the rabbi's keeping it a secret. I've

helped them memorize their speeches at home, though. And their Hebrew has improved, too."

"Why do they have to memorize anything—that's so stilted. Can't they use notes?"

"No."

As if on cue, Lester and Larry push their way into the social hall.

"Hi, Aunt Ruby."

Essie Sue insists that they call me *aunt*—I know from my own childhood that this is a Southern thing, although maybe it's universal, and it's supposed to be more familiar than calling me Ms. Rothman, but less familiar than just Ruby. It always makes me squirm.

"Hi, guys. What's up?"

"The rabbi says Jackie's ahead of us on her Bat Mitzvah studies and we have to catch up," Larry says.

"Yeah," Lester says. "Why do we have to be up there with a girl, anyway? They're always smarter. And taller."

"Look at it this way, boys—if she weren't up there sharing everything, you'd have to do even more. And your speeches would probably have to be even longer."

They look at each other as if maybe this is something worth considering. I get silence as a reply, which from Larry and Lester is praise indeed.

I want to drop in on Kevin, so before Essie Sue can think of more work for me, I use the kids' arrival as an excuse to vamoose.

Kevin's in his study, downing a can of Mountain Dew.

"Ha—I can see why you need the biggest caffeine shot a tin can offer," I say.

"There are bigger," he says, "but this is all I've got. Want one?"

"No thanks. Coffee keeps me edgy enough. Is this thing really going to happen?"

"Oh yeah," he says. "I can't say it's going well, but

what's the alternative? Can you see me telling Essie Sue the Bar Mitzvah has to be postponed?"

"I see your point. Did you write their speeches, or what?"

"Well, I got nothing when I asked them to produce something, so I decided to interview them and take notes on what they were interested in."

"Which was?"

"Sports, CDs, and video games."

"In other words, what everybody else is interested in at that age."

"I zeroed in on sports ethics," he says. "And I pulled some stuff out of them. What they'd want done to them and what they would think was unfair—things like that."

"I think that's brilliant. There ought to be plenty to relate to in their Torah readings."

"Well, don't overestimate what they took in from these sessions. I decided that *short* was the name of the game here, you'll pardon the pun."

"How about their Hebrew?"

"If you can get through the Buda, Texas, inflections and relate that to known Hebrew, you might be able to understand them. I was more interested in not having any more wrestling demonstrations from them. I proposed a bribe."

I'm more and more impressed—I didn't know Kevin was this versatile.

"I told them I'd take them to a Cowboys game if they worked with me on their speeches and their Hebrew. I also mentioned that they might have to take the year's work over if they didn't make an effort. Since they want to go out for football next year, I had their attention."

"How's Jackie doing?"

"I'd say she could already qualify as a teacher to Larry and Lester. I'm a little worried that Essie Sue will think

I've given her the best parts, but the truth is that she's at such a different level. Her speech is top-notch."

"Oh, don't worry about that—Essie Sue won't be that discerning. Unfortunately, she's only tuned to the two F's—Food and Fashion. If the twins' huskies fit them and the table looks good, you won't hear *boo* from Essie Sue."

I'm feeling for him all of a sudden. "I'll be impressed, though, Kevin—you've gotten more out of them than I would have imagined. I hope they come through for you."

"Thanks, Ruby. I'll be glad when this week is over, whatever happens."

I walk out of his study crossing my fingers—it's the *whatever* that bothers me.

chapter
47

....

Constant shampoos at home and two special treat-
ments at the hair salon give me the illusion of not smelling
like a lox as I walk into Temple Rita on the big triple crown
day. Between the regular temple-goers, Rose's friends, and
the people Essie Sue's managed to strong-arm, the place is
bulging. Even Ed has promised to try and make it in time
for the reception—he can't leave San Antonio early
enough to attend services. Someone passes me a program,
and I see that Kevin has succumbed to Essie Sue's demand
for a processional.

Rose has saved me a seat. She's looking both happy and
sad as she sits with her husband, Ray—I know she must be
thinking of her father and how much he'd want to be here to
see Jackie. Since Rose has refused to make a show, the field
is left to the most persistent, and we're treated to the specta-
cle of Essie Sue, holding down a funereal twin on each arm
as she smiles her way down the aisle. Larry and Lester, entirely out of character in their black suits, look petrified but
resigned to their fate. Kevin brings up the rear with Jackie
by his side. She's wearing a beautiful pale yellow dress, and

her long, brown hair hangs in a ponytail laced with a matching yellow ribbon. You'd never know she's only thirteen.

Kevin conducts the service up to the point where Jackie, Larry, and Lester are scheduled to take over. Jackie's part of the Hebrew portion is flawless, which doesn't surprise me, and I lean over to pat Rose on the shoulder. She and Ray are beaming, but I'm personally waiting for the other shoe to drop.

I don't have long to worry. Essie Sue, who seems to be carrying a long list containing the order of the service and who has appointed herself chief prompter, pokes each twin in the arm almost as soon as Jackie chants her last words. The boys sprint to their places and begin reading the Hebrew in unison.

"That's unusual, to say the least," I whisper to Rose.

"The rabbi couldn't get anything out of them until he told them they could read together," she says. "Apparently it relaxed both of them."

"Are they giving the same speech, too?"

"I'm not sure," she says.

It seems that the twins have taken care of that, too. Following Jackie's well-thought-out address, their speech is, as promised, about being fair on the football field. They've decided to split the talk in half. First Larry rushes through his version of sports ethics, and then Lester recites the follow-up. They don't seem to have made the usual attempt to tie their theme to the weekly Torah portion, but I figure Kevin knew when to stop. Nothing about the speech is quotable, which in this case is probably a good thing.

Essie Sue is visibly thrilled, as are the Bitman twins, one of whom is the boys' mother, I keep having to remind myself. Aptly, she and her husband are relegated to a bit part in this event, but what did they expect? In my opinion, Kevin's the real hero here, merely for bringing this off without anything catastrophic happening—at least not yet.

He's nowhere near as sanguine as I am, though. I see him glued to his chair—biting his fingernails and tapping his wing tips. I'm quite sure he's thinking that it ain't over till it's over.

Miraculously, there *is* a first-round finish, and I even find myself enjoying Essie Sue's recessional out of the sanctuary and into the Blumberg Social Hall for the reception.

Larry and Lester, having acted with restraint for two hours more than their bodies were built for, kick off the reception with a spontaneous game of bagel Frisbee.

"But they have to stand in line and receive compliments," Essie Sue yells. "Go get them, Ruby."

"Quit while you're ahead, Essie Sue. There's no way you're going to rein them in at this point. You shake the hands."

Or appoint anyone, as long as it's not me. I OD'd on the meeting and greeting when I was married to Stu, and now I won't come within ten feet of a receiving line.

"I'll just have to let the Bitman sisters represent our family," Essie Sue says. "I'm needed to keep the flow going at the reception tables. Besides, I want to check on your partner, Milt—his catering skills leave a lot to be desired."

"Milt's doing fine, Essie Sue. He's knocked himself out getting the platters ready and setting up the baked goods for you."

"So far, so good," she says. "And speaking of baked goods, I have a small surprise he doesn't know about."

Oy. I hope she hasn't tried some so-called gourmet recipe at home—this is a woman who's always paid for her culinary successes, not cooked them. We're all better off if she keeps it that way.

Even though I'm not going through the line, I stop and tap Jackie on the back as she receives congratulations with her parents—they all look happy and relieved.

"You were great, honey."

"We're so proud of her, Ruby," Rose says.

"Just be careful," I say. "Essie Sue tells me she has a special surprise."

"Surviving a joint ceremony with the boys is reward enough," Rose says. "I'm appreciative of Essie Sue's generosity in including us, but we don't need any of her surprises."

I feel an arm around my waist, and turn to see Ed right where I want him to be—close to me.

"Hi, babe," I say, giving him a quick kiss. "I'm so glad you made it."

"Did I miss any theater of the absurd? No clash of the Titans?"

"Clashes were at a minimum," I tell him. "Really. The service was amazingly trouble-free."

"How did the lox turn out?"

"The platters look wonderful, thanks to Milt. I'm glad we stayed miles away from the Steuben delicacies."

"Did Essie Sue carry out her threat to negotiate with them for a lower price? I had the feeling she thought it was your fault they didn't provide the food, after all the hype about going up there to order the best of the best."

"Of course she thought I was to blame—what else is new? And it *was* our fault, but for good reason. No, I would have definitely called you if she had been in touch with them. As soon as I told her about the new fish order being a bargain, she concentrated on the dessert table."

Ed points across the room. "Speaking of the sweets table, what's going on over there?"

We go closer, to see better. Essie Sue is standing at the baked goods table, directly behind the ice sculpture spelling out the letters *BM*. For Bar and Bat Mitzvah, I presume. She's clinking glasses—always a bad sign.

"Ladies and gentlemen, may I have your attention please?"

Getting this mob to notice anything is going to take more than a clink—which is what bothers me. All of a sudden I'm filled with a sense of dread far beyond what the occasion calls for, even considering Essie Sue's previous potential for catastrophe. I dig my fingers into Ed's arm.

She does it, though, shouting loudly enough to penetrate the lunchtime din and make herself heard in the far corners of the hall.

"As you all know," she says, "we've invited Larry and Lester's classmate Jackie to celebrate with us today."

I give Ed a look. "Please don't tell me she's going to embarrass Rose and Ray by saying she paid for the whole reception."

"She couldn't," he says.

"Yes, she could, but maybe she won't."

"I'd like to have Jackie step up here," Essie Sue says.

I see a reluctant Jackie being gently *noodged* forward by the crowd. Even Larry and Lester stop their game of tag on the periphery of the room to gawk as Essie Sue gestures for Jackie to join her behind the table. I see Rose and Ray watching warily from the side—I don't blame them.

"A gift?" I ask Ed. He shrugs.

Essie Sue turns to a service cart parked just behind her, and lifts a white cardboard box from the cart to the table. She opens the box and slides out a round dark chocolate cake, top-heavy with icing and overdecorated to the extreme. No surprise, considering who's presenting it.

"This is for you, Jackie." She reads the inscription for the crowd:

"TO JACKIE, FOR HER BAT MITZVAH. CONGRATULATIONS.

"This was a special shipment, packed in dry ice," Essie Sue announces. "It came with instructions for you to have the very first bite."

Essie Sue cuts the cake and fills a fork with the first bite. Jackie, leaning over so as not to drop chocolate on her pale yellow dress, has that deer-in-the-headlights look of a teenager who would rather be anywhere but facing this woman who's shoving a fork in her mouth.

"This comes from your relatives who couldn't be here," she says.

Things happen so fast I can't absorb them all. First, Larry and Lester race toward the table, bumping it hard enough to knock Essie Sue backward.

"No fair, no fair!" This shriek is in unison, no less.

"It's our Bar Mitzvah, too," Lester says.

"You know chocolate's our favorite," Larry tells Essie Sue, who's only preoccupied with the big brown smear that's just appeared on her pink linen suit.

I'm not too far from Rose during all the ruckus, and she catches my eye.

"We don't have relatives who couldn't come," she says to us.

I look at Ed, and without a word to each other, we start running, doing a nosedive toward the sweets table. My priority is to grab a surprised Jackie around the waist and pull her away from the cake altogether. Ed grabs Essie Sue's hand in case she automatically licks it where the forkful of chocolate had been. And we both scream to the black-suited twins, who fortunately have, out of respect for the occasion, restrained themselves from sticking their hands into the cake.

chapter
48

....

E-mail from: Ruby
To: Nan
Subject: *Strychnine*

Thanks for your Net search on strychnine—I'd done a quick one myself, but not as thorough as yours. Gustav Steuben apparently didn't worry about the bitter taste of the poison—he'd loaded the cake with so much of the stuff that by the time Jackie had taken a first bite, she'd have had it. As I told you the other night, the hardest thing we had to do at the scene was to corral the Levee twins—bulls would have been easier to steer away from the food. I was desperately afraid they'd sample that icing while Ed and I were holding back Jackie and Essie Sue.

Meanwhile, Essie Sue has made the little darlings into hometown heroes, and I have to admit that without their interference in rushing the table to get some of that cake, we'd have had no chance to stop Essie Sue from feeding that forkful of poisoned cake to Jackie. So much for good manners. Of course, none of this would have happened if

Essie Sue hadn't given one call to the Steubens to try to negotiate a price with them. She never told us about that, and Jackie almost paid with her life.

I'm pooped, but by all means continue to ask me questions about stuff I've forgotten to tell you.

....

E-mail from: Nan
To: Ruby
Subject: *Mr. Sam*

Are they charging the other brother—Mr. Sam? I get it about Gustav, but I'm wondering what you think Sam's motives were? Do you believe him?

Another question. Until you and Ed visited the Steubens' plant, Gustav didn't know about the Bat Mitzvah, right? And when he found out, his hatred of Herman Guenther made him want to wipe out the progeny, too?

....

E-mail from: Ruby
To: Nan
Subject: *Answers*

Yes, Gustav and the family felt so betrayed that Herman had put Bertie's life in danger without telling them, they carried the bitterness all those years. But of course, they didn't know where Herman was until they moved to New Jersey and saw that Zabar's newsletter. That was when Gustav sent the postcard that frightened Herman, and soon, Herman decided to retire and be with his family in Texas.

To answer your other question, Sam has been fully cooperating with the police. Sam hasn't been indicted yet for Herman's murder or for the attempted murder of Jackie—Paul says the police don't think Sam wanted to kill Herman, and certainly not Jackie. I don't think so, either.

After all, his information enabled the police to capture Gustav.

••

E-mail from: Nan
To: Ruby
Subject: *??*

You said Herman ran refugees from the northern part of Germany to southern Denmark. How? Did he volunteer?

••

E-mail from: Ruby
To: Nan
Subject: *More*

Okay, you already know they were living in that country village in Denmark when WWII started. Bertie was living with her mother, father, and the two brothers. Herman was apparently living in a boardinghouse, working with the brothers in their smokehouse, and engaged to Bertie. The family wasn't Jewish, but didn't mind the thought of Herman marrying Bertie.

We think Herman was somehow recruited by the Underground, since he was in a perfect position to help smuggle out the Jewish refugees. He was well known and trusted in the countryside, and he lived with non-Jews. Maybe no one even knew he was Jewish—we aren't sure. Anyway, he kept his Underground activities secret from the Steuben family and probably from everyone, even Bertie. As the war progressed, he was, I'm sure, drawn in more and more, and it was dangerous work. From what Sam has told us, at some point Herman decided to recruit Bertie and enlist her help in smuggling someone across the border. Someone on the other side found out and planted a bomb in Bertie's bedroom. Maybe they also assumed Herman slept there with her.

The family didn't discover until after the war that Bertie was killed because of Herman. The fact that she wasn't a Jew had made her participation especially galling to the other side, and almost guaranteed a vicious punishment. The brothers were, as I said, beyond furious with Herman for taking advantage of his position with the family and endangering Bertie's life. I don't believe the fact that this was good work even made a dent at that point—they simply felt that he was responsible for their impressionable sister's death.

••

E-mail from: Ruby
To: Nan
Subject: *P.S.*

Forgot to say that we didn't tell the Steubens about the Bat Mitzvah—Essie Sue did, when she called their company to try and negotiate a price behind our backs. You know how yakkity she is—she told them about Herman dying, and the poor grandchild, and who knows what else. I can just imagine Gustav's reaction on the other end of the phone when he realized Herman had a granddaughter who was thriving.

chapter
49

·········

By closing time every night, Milt has usually changed into his leather slippers for the cleanup—his feet can't take it. Tonight, he's at the big kitchen table sipping a mug of new espresso roast and using a wooden crate as a footstool. I take three steaming rye bagels out of the oven for Milt, me, and Paul Lundy. I've learned to love these plain, with no toppings to spoil the tangy taste of the rye. Milt and Paul both prefer cream cheese, and they've served themselves already from the refrigerator.

"So how was your trip East, Lundy?" Milt's talking and chewing his first bite at the same time. I don't blame him— when the bagel's hot, that first bite is the best.

"I like Eternal," Paul says. "Sue me. The world up there revolves around the commute—I couldn't take those rush hours. We got in and out pretty fast, though—the whole trip only took four days, including the interviews."

"Ruby tells me Sam Steuben led you to his brother."

"Well, to be more exact, Sam led the New Jersey police to his brother. If that roundup hadn't been so neat before we came, our stay would have been a lot longer. We interviewed Sam as soon as we got there—he was in police custody. We'd called the authorities right from the Temple reception, and when they went to the plant, Sam told them everything. Gustav had emptied their joint bank account and was caught at the JFK airport, about to board a plane for Frankfurt. We don't know where he was going from there, but he still had friends in Denmark, so who knows?"

I'm feeling mellow after the Jewish soul food, and tempted to just listen, but of course I have to jump in.

"Sam was never a part of the plan to murder Herman," I say. "He carried an awful grudge, too, but he wasn't a killer. Gustav did frequent Internet searches on Herman, mostly looking for his last-known address, and when he stumbled on the *Eternal Ear* photos and article Essie Sue had put out, he wanted Sam to fly down to the Austin airport with him. Just to talk, he said, but Sam refused, worrying that something more would happen. So when Gustav finally did go down to Eternal, he didn't tell Sam until he returned."

Milt's curiosity is almost as great as mine—it's one of the things I love about him. And Paul, when he's in the right mood, can be incredibly patient about our incessant questions. I love that, too. Lately, Paul's been especially easy to talk to, and tonight we're all melding nicely. Because Milt knows so much less than I do about this, I can relax and let him test Paul's limits instead of getting in trouble myself.

"Gustav told Sam he knifed Herman?" Milt asks.

"Yep," Paul says. "He took a cab to the house, rang the bell, and changed his mind about showing himself when Herman answered the door. He hid in the bushes, and during the time Herman stayed outside looking around, Gustav ran around to the back. Sam was unclear about what his brother was going to do at that point. Possibly he wanted to go inside through the back porch and then surprise Herman, or maybe he was ready to choke him—Gustav is a huge, strong man. Sam didn't know if he had a weapon with him. Anyway, it turns out that Herman himself supplied the weapon—the slicing knife he was going to use to cut the lox. Gustav obviously found the knife at the table on the porch, took it, and waited for the couple of minutes it would have taken for Herman to return. Then he acted."

"That couple of minutes could mean the difference between premeditation and killing out of fury when he saw Herman," I say.

Milt picks up where I leave off. "What did he say when you interviewed him?"

"Nada. He's said very little, but Sam has made up for it."

"Well, there's no doubt about Jackie's cake being carefully planned," Milt says. "Wasn't killing Herman enough?"

"Sam says he wanted Herman's line to be wiped out. Or maybe it was just more retribution. We might never know for sure. You could make the case that expecting Rose to eat the cake would have been irrational, but then, the whole scheme's irrational."

"So Gustav told Sam everything?" I say.

Paul apparently hasn't lost patience yet. "After Ruby and Ed left, Sam told us he pressed his brother for more answers. That was the point when Gustav told him he'd been in Texas when he'd supposedly been checking out a business deal in Connecticut, and that Herman wasn't a factor in their lives anymore. I'm sure Gustav had been dying to tell his brother what he'd accomplished."

"Sam was scared to turn him in?" I say.

"He thought about it, but he couldn't bring himself to do it, partially because he'd been so distraught about Bertie's death himself through the years. Gustav's idea about the cake, of course, came when Essie Sue called him about the Bat Mitzvah. I'm pretty sure Sam knew about that, too, but he was afraid by that time for his own life if he told."

"Yeah," I say, "and the irony is that if we'd confided in

Essie Sue about the Steubens when we came back from New Jersey, she might never have called them."

Milt pours one more round of coffee—I take half a cup, but Paul passes. "By the way, Paul," Milt says, "Ruby told me we'll be asked to make statements about Acme Jobbers, our former distributors. Grace wants to know if it's safe."

"Tell your wife not to worry," Paul says. "They're finished. I wish I could have discovered the extent of their mob connections, but I guess we can't have everything. The IRS is involved now, and the people managing those processing plants are doing a lot of talking."

"Herman was right about them," I tell Milt, "but obviously, they didn't kill him. I think they were shocked to hear that he was murdered and wanted to do everything they could to keep me from looking into their affairs. They've admitted frightening us when we stayed at the gold mine."

"I'm just glad you were only there one night," Paul says. "You know Ruby," he says to Milt—"with more time, she might have provoked them into more serious intimidation."

"Back to Essie Sue," I say. "If she hadn't cluelessly put Herman's life on the Internet, none of this might have happened."

Paul reaches out and brushes his hand against mine on the table. At least I think that's what he just did—it was so fast I'm not certain.

"You're just trying to deflect our attention from your own risk-taking, Ruby. But don't sweat it about Essie Sue—who knows if the woman is more dangerous when she's informed or uninformed?"

I'm about to speculate, but my cell phone rings. It's Ed.

"Hi," I say.

"You've got company," he guesses.

I can't decide whether to make a thing out of this and go to a more private place, or to stay where I am. I stay, but I can tell that both Milt and Paul know it's Ed, anyway.

"This won't take long if you're busy," Ed says. "I know you won't want to hear this, but as soon as I write up the first of the Herman Guenther stories for the paper, they're sending me on another long assignment to Sonora—a big investigation we're doing about NAFTA. So I'm afraid our plans are on hold."

"Just like that?"

"Sorry, honey—I just found out. I know you can't talk."

He sounds thrilled I can't talk. As well he should be.

I give as generic a good-bye as I can, considering my audience. I try to rearrange my face into a neutral expression, which has never worked before and doesn't work now. Another lonesome summer.

"How's Ed?" Milt asks, giving Paul what I consider to be a very peculiar look. I wonder if these two ever talk. Like guys, I mean.

"Great," I say.

"Do you two have plans for the future?" Paul says. I know he'd never have the nerve to ask me this if we were alone, and it irks me. But then, almost anything would irk me at the moment. Besides, I don't know the answer to that question, and that *really* irks me.

"Never mind," he says—a dismissal, not an apology, I notice, but it somehow comes off sounding decent. Then, he really floors me.

"If you're ever feeling like company," he adds almost offhandedly, "would you want to have dinner sometime?"

recipes
....

Ruby's Lox and Scrambled Eggs

3 tbsp. butter
¼ onion, chopped
2 large slices lox, cut into strips
6 eggs
2 tbsp. capers

Melt the butter in a frying pan and sauté the chopped onion, then add the lox pieces. Whisk the eggs in a bowl and then scramble with the other ingredients in the pan until the mixture reaches the desired consistency. Garnish with the capers.

SERVES 3.

Milt's Scooped Lox and Bagel

1 bagel, halved
2 slices lox, finely cut
4 tbsp. softened cream cheese

Scoop out the bagel halves. Fill with a mixure of the lox and cream cheese. Serve with strong coffee, orange juice, and the Sunday *Times* for a weekend brunch to remember.

Essie Sue's Low-Fat Lox Treat

2 paper-thin slices lox
1/16 tsp. diet butter or 1/2 teaspoon nonfat cream cheese
2 unsalted, unflavored Ry-Krisp crackers

Place the lox slices under running water for 3 minutes to wash off any oils.

Pat dry between paper towels to remove even more fat or oil.

Spread diet butter or nonfat cream cheese over the crackers with a thin knife.

Top with the thoroughly cleansed lox slices.

Enjoy with a vintage bottle of water and a copy of *Weight Watchers* magazine.

SERVES 2.

About the Author

Sharon Kahn has worked as an arbitrator, attorney, and freelance writer. She is a graduate of Vassar College and the University of Arizona Law School. The mother of three, and the former wife of a rabbi, she lives in Austin, Texas. *Fax Me a Bagel,* a Ruby, the Rabbi's Wife novel and her mystery debut, appeared in 1998. It was followed by *Never Nosh a Matzo Ball* and *Don't Cry for Me, Hot Pastrami.*